Flying

Peter finished at the far side of the room, then it was our turn to jump. Summer tapped my arm. "This is it, kid!"

Here came the music. Now was the time. Summer and I took off together. I stretched my legs into a full split, sailed, landed without jerking, and leaped again.

Suddenly, I was Cynthia Gregory flying through *Don Quixote*. My pilot light flamed. Fire blossomed through my body. I was dancing! Really dancing!

When we finished, Summer and I grinned at each other. Her eyes shimmered. She slapped the palms of her hands against both of mine.

"We did it, girl! We really did it! The super fantastic team of Lara Havas and Summer Jones is on its way. Watch out, New York!"

point

A Time To Dance

Karen Strickler Dean

SCHOLASTIC INC.
New York Toronto London Auckland Sydney

*For Lucie and Tom
and my friend Alice Soard*

Acknowledgments

Special thanks to Carmen DeArce for her part in inspiring this novel in the first place and to Barbara Shulman for helping with the Hungarian background.

Also thanks to the following people for patiently listening to various parts of the book: Thelma Shaw, Shirley Bollock, Kathy Pelta, Shirley Climo, Ellen McKenzie, Barbara Shulman, Ella Gibson, and Stella Neuer.

Sincere appreciation to Ruth Cohen for her encouragement while I was writing *A Time To Dance*.

Chapter 1

Almost nothing tonight was the same. Not the ballet class fifteen of us were waiting along the barres to take. Not the storm lashing the tall Victorian house where our ballet school fills the first floor.

Two things remained unchanged for me, though. Loving ballet. But also loving Peter.

I frowned and chewed a straggle of brownish hair that had escaped from my topknot. But I refused to look across the studio at Peter. I would die if he caught me staring at him. Finally, though, I peeked at his reflection in the mirror at the front of the big studio. Golly, he stood so tall, so sturdy, astride legs thick as marble columns. They gleamed moon-white under the florescent lamps because, unlike the rest of us, he doesn't wear tights. He hasn't since weight lifting developed his legs into such pillars.

Just looking at him sent shivers of excitement through me. Peter is six feet but not skinny like when he first came here two years ago. No, dancing and pumping iron, as he calls it, have built him a solid physique from his staunch neck to his broad feet in canvas ballet slippers.

Suddenly in the mirror the clear green of his eyes wavered. Had he seen me peering at him? My face burned. I flapped a leg up behind me, tensed it, and pretended I was looking in the glass only to study the long, long line of my *arabesque*. But his gaze wasn't on me. It was on the pointy upturned face of giggling Meredith. She clung to him, linked both arms around his tapered waist. Her laugh whinnied above the slosh of rain on the bay windows and above the wind screaming through the porch that wraps around the house.

My throat ached. I turned away and tied my dingy sweater tighter at the waist. Forget Peter! Dancing was more important. Especially tonight! This wasn't our regular advanced class. It was the first of two auditions for scholarships back in New York. And I absolutely had to make this one. If I didn't I wouldn't even get a chance at the second.

I grasped the holy medal Mom gave me last month on my sixteenth birthday. I stroked my thumb along the tiny figure of Our Lady. She rises out of a button-sized gold oval and dangles under my leotard on a chain between my breasts. I hunched my shoulders and squeezed the medal harder.

Please help me to really dance tonight, Blessed Mother. Let me be super strong.

But somebody kept twitching my left legwarmer.

"Shoot, Lara, I'm tired of yelling at you over this storm. Quit daydreaming."

My eyes turned toward a familiar ringing voice. On the floor nearly under my feet sprawled Summer Jones, my best friend since fifth grade. She was limbering up her turnout. Inside pink legwarmers, her legs angled forward in a long triangle. Her knees flapped up and down like pistons. She blew a huge lavender bubble. The air filled with its sweet grapey odor.

"Hmm? What did you say?" I asked, blinking.

"I said, tell me the instant the man from New York comes in so I can get to my place at the barre. The audition'll start any minute."

I sighed. "I know."

"For Lord's sake, at a time like this, quit worrying about Peter!"

I lifted my chin. "What makes you think I'm even thinking about him?"

"When aren't you?" Summer asked. "Anyway, now you've got to concentrate on the audition. *Focus*, as Stephanie says."

Stephanie is beautiful, black Stephanie Martin. We had her for fifth grade at East-side Elementary before she quit classroom teaching and took over the intermediate classes at Markoff's Ballet School. Eleventh graders now, Summer and I have been studying here for six years.

Summer giggled up at me and rolled her eyes. They changed from tan to gold so I knew she was coming out with something really crazy. "Lord, did you hear what I just said? *Focus!* Living with Stephanie is making me sound as teacherish as she does. I'm getting so I spout her so-called Standard English even when she isn't around."

I shrugged. With the audition about to begin, who wanted to discuss Stephanie Martin's mania for correct grammar! Her mother used to drill it into her, she told us, and she sure drilled it into all her fifth graders. Especially into Summer, a black kid originally from North Carolina, and me, whose family is from Hungary. "Forget Mrs. Martin," I said. "This audition is really getting to me. Feel how cold my hands are."

I touched Summer's arm with my long white fingers. She flinched.

"Lord, they're icicles. Like the hands of a snow queen. I'm not exactly laid-back tonight, either. I've got a dozen butterflies mixing it up down in my belly."

She giggled, patted her flat stomach, and rolled onto her spine. She pedaled her feet in the air and started laughing. Really cracking up. Her eyes turned golden again. They nearly matched the tiny rings in her ears.

"My butterflies are doing *brisés*, I think, girl. But we've got to get hold of ourselves.

And you've got to take off that raggedy sweater, Lara, and do something about your hair."

I put hand to head. Most of my hair had slithered out of its topknot and down to my shoulders. That was nothing new. My hair never stays put. It's straight and slippery, not silky and wavy like Meredith's blonde mane.

I would have to fasten my topknot all over again. I gave my head a toss. Bobby pins spun everywhere and pinged all over the floor.

Summer groaned. "Not again!"

She leaped up, spanked the dust and rosin off her rear end, and began plunging after my bobby pins. I started looking, too, pivoting in slow circles, and blinking into the cracks between the narrow brown floor boards.

"Lord, you're something else, Lara Havas," Summer said. "Like Mama says, 'That chile just drift round. Go whichever way the wind decide to blow her.'"

I rounded my shoulders. I mean, it sounded like my own mom putting me down for not paying attention or for not remembering to do my homework or for dressing sort of sloppy. "Tuck in your blouse, Lara. My saints, you want the sisters sending home another note about you never looking neat at school?"

"Course Stephanie calls your walk willowy. Willowy and languid," Summer went on. "I say it's sexy."

"Sexy?" I asked, astonished. Pleased, though. I blushed and wondered if Peter thought my walk was sexy, too. I imagined his eyes and quick, shy smile gleaming at me and him maybe saying, "Hey, Lara, that walk of yours is all right!"

I couldn't keep from looking across the room at him. But I shouldn't have. For right in front of all those kids waiting along the barres for the audition to begin, Meredith was nibbling Peter's ear.

If Summer noticed, she didn't let on. She just handed me a half dozen bobby pins and laughed. "Your walk's not as sexy as Stephanie's though, Lara. Not yet," she added, then stood watching while, with shaky fingers, I pinned up my hair again.

"What you could do, Lara," Summer said with a roll of her eyes, "is chop it off short. Get a perm. Wear it in an afro like mine and Stephanie's, even if you ain't black like us."

She patted her cap of reddish-brown hair, blew another grapey bubble, then slurped it back into her mouth.

"That would make us practically twins," she said. "Except for you being so tall. And so sooo white!"

She held out a nut-brown arm. Alongside hers, mine looked washed-out and as thin-skinned as my father's. *No wonder I'm always turning red, especially around Peter! All he has to do is grin and say "Hey, Lara!" and my face goes scarlet.*

Now lightning flashed into the studio and passed through a leaded glass circle in the bay window behind us. It painted red and green swirls on Summer's face and flickered the florescent lamps above us. Thunder followed immediately, thudded and rolled along the gabled roof. I drew in my shoulders. Summer chewed her gum hard.

"Lord, girl, you must've been praying up a storm! Get it? Praying up a storm?"

I caught in my breath. Good thing Mom hadn't heard. She would claim that was blasphemy, a mortal sin. She's always thought Summer is a bad influence on me and blames her for getting me into ballet, which Mom calls "a bunch of foolishness. Worse than the folk dancing your father did back in Hungary." But it was really Mrs. Martin's after-school dance club at Eastside Elementary that started my interest in ballet. Passion, I guess you'd call it.

I just have to dance even if I'm only in the *corps de ballet* and never become famous like Cynthia Gregory, my favorite ballerina. Maybe it sounds strange but I think of my passion as a pilot light, like the one in our old gas oven at home. Mine burns in a sort of niche below my rib cage. Usually the flame is tiny and blue. Sometimes, though, it flares as hot and white as the lightning tonight. When that happens, I stop flopping around like the rag doll I keep on my bed and become strong and sure and really dance.

Let that happen tonight, Blessed Mother. Help me concentrate. Let me be super super strong.

Lightning speared through the windows again. Thunder shook the house. I covered my ears. Summer grabbed hold of me. She was giggling and trembling at the same time.

"Cut it out, Lara. Quit your praying. Enough is enough!"

But when the thunder faded to a mutter, she added, "Guess it's just fanfare for the man from New York. Here he comes now. Da-DAH!"

Chapter 2

The man from New York bounced into the classroom and plopped his fat bottom on a narrow folding chair. Behind him came Alex Markoff, who owns this school and teaches our advanced class. Unlike the man from New York, he is still lean and muscular.

Last of all Stephanie Martin glided into the room. She moved so smoothly that she might have been wearing roller skates instead of spike-heeled suede pumps.

"Oops," Summer whispered, poking her purple bubble gum under one of the barre supports, "better to park my wad now before old Stephanie spots it and explodes."

Mrs. Martin smoothed her beige wool skirt under her, then settled on a chair near the piano. She crossed one magenta-stockinged knee over the other and, curling her long, magenta-tipped fingers together, folded her hands on her knee. She shot a glance at Summer and me, then looked away — but not before my stomach knotted. One of her beautiful, high-arched feet twitched back and forth, back and forth.

Mr. Markoff cleared his throat. "Ladies and gentlemen, we are privileged to have with us tonight, Greg Landon. He and I were principal dancers together with New York Ballet Association. He's traveling all over the country looking for talented students between the ages of thirteen and eighteen to try out for scholarship classes at NYBA's school."

I pulled a lock of hair into my mouth. Did I have enough talent to win? I shivered as an icy draft blasted under a crack in the bay window behind me.

"The final audition takes place in New York this coming April," Mr. Markoff was saying. "We're happy Greg could fit us into his schedule even on a Sunday night during the worst storm in years. Really, Greg, this weather is very unusual for San José, even in January."

Mr. Markoff tapped his cane on the floor and nodded to the pianist. Mr. Swensen's old hands trembled above the keyboard but he took time to smile over at Summer and me. Which was more than Stephanie Martin did. She just kept swinging that foot of hers.

The music began. I took a deep breath. The air smelled of rain, sweat, eucalyptus from the grove behind the house, and the baby powder we all had layered on in the dressing room.

In front of me Summer gripped the barre

so hard that her knuckles pointed up into tiny peaks. "Lord," she whispered over her shoulder, "now those butterflies of mine are doing *grands jetés*."

My own stomach was churning, too. After we completed *demi-pliés* on one side, Mr. Markoff stopped us. "Peter," he said, "when you point your toes, don't let them turn in. You tend to sickle."

I sighed. I sure hoped Peter made it to New York, too.

In front of me Summer pulled in her rear and tried to force her legs straight out to the sides. She's not as limber as I am, but her technique is stronger.

We both got through the barre work okay, though, except that I wobbled a *rond de jambe* exercise on *pointe*. Mr. Markoff tapped his cane against my stomach. "Balance by pulling up here, Lara." Blushing, I quickly sucked it in.

"Watch your turn-out," Mr. Markoff told Summer. I saw her back stiffen and her hand tighten on the barre.

After barre exercises we lined up in the center of the studio. It used to be two rooms: a parlor and a dining room. Mr. Markoff tore down the partition between them when he bought the house. He left two thick redwood pillars, though, to support the ceiling.

Now he was calling off steps for the first *adagio*. "*Croisé devant*. No, Summer, face the left corner. *Développé*. It's not necessary to extend your leg clear to the ceiling,

Lara. Next, around to second. Hips down, everybody. To the rear. *Arabesque*. Into *attitude*. *Relevé*. Balance. Back to fifth. Let's see it."

I gulped. Balance! *Oh, please let my balance be okay tonight!*

I unfolded my right leg into a steep forward *développé*, circled it ear-high to the side, then rotated it to the rear. My legs were moving easily, as if I had just oiled them. I was dancing nearly as smoothly as Cynthia Gregory, wasn't I?

Remembering her in the Siren role in *The Prodigal Son*, I straightened my back, arched my neck, fluttered my eyelids, and curled my lips in a sexy smile. I was imagining that Peter was my partner when somebody poked me. "Psst!" Summer whispered. "We're on the other leg now."

I blinked around. Good grief, I still had my right leg lifted while the other kids were all extending their lefts. Sweat soaked my leotard. I switched legs and hoped nobody had noticed. Not Peter or the man from New York or Stephanie Martin, either. She's always yelling at me to concentrate, just like my mother. Only Mom isn't talking about concentrating on ballet. She wants me to quit ballet and plan on becoming something practical like a teacher or a nurse.

Summer jabbed me with her elbow. "Pay attention, Lara," she whispered. "Mr. Markoff's showing the next combination."

I gave myself a shake. *Pirouettes!* I sucked

12

a strand of hair. Even on good days my *pirouettes* aren't much.

But when the music began, I slid into second position, bent my knees in a *plié*, and took off into a series of turns.

Single. Double. Triple, I said to myself while I spun. *Now repeat. Single. Double. Triple.*

And I did them! I did all the *pirouettes*. I kept my balance, spun, and landed each turn perfectly.

Poor Summer didn't, though. She wobbled her turns, hopped the landings, and did two sets of double *pirouettes* when Mr. Markoff wanted the last to be a triple.

"Oh, man!" she muttered to herself. Her eyes brimmed with tears. "And look at Meredith spin."

I scowled at the whirling blur. But I couldn't think about her now. Mr. Markoff was demonstrating a combination of beats that looked impossible. I mean, why didn't I leave right now? Summer must have seen my panic.

"Cool it, Lara," she whispered beside me. "I'll help you while Meredith's group is doing the combination."

Summer led me to a corner near one of the bay windows. Rain swooshed down the panes.

"Follow along behind me," she said.

I tried but my long, skinny feet wouldn't cross and recross nimbly like Summer's small ones. We went over and over the combination until Mr. Markoff called us up front to dance. Our group included Summer, me, and the three boys in the class. One of whom, of course, was Peter.

Mr. Markoff said, "Remember, Lara, lift from the waist. Watch your turnout, Summer. Simon and Clarence, since you're new here and not used to beats, leave them out. And, Peter, you'll jump higher if you *plié* before you try to get off the floor. Ready, begin."

We took off into the first *brisé* like *fecskék*, as Apa, my father, might say. *Fecskék* means swallows in Hungarian. Apa means father. Apa used to write poetry in Hungary.

Well, tonight, thanks to Summer's coaching, I danced the combination more or less like a swallow the first time. Not when we had to do it again, though. Then I lost the tempo, forgot the steps, and had to fake the ending. I scrambled into the final pose nearly crying.

I frowned down at the floor boards. Everybody must be staring at me. Especially Peter and creepy Meredith!

But Summer came and pulled me back to the barre. "It wasn't all that bad, Lara," she whispered. "Really!"

I sniffed but managed to keep from actually crying until I saw Peter looking at me. Red-faced, a frown between his eyes, he seemed about to smile and say, "Hey, Lara, don't feel bad!" But then Meredith clutched his arm and led him away. I fled to the rosin box near one of the windows. Wind and rain slammed against the dark glass. In it, I saw my head drooping forward and the round bone at the back of my neck protruding like a golf ball.

Standing in the rosin box, I rubbed the ends of my *pointe* shoes in the yellow powder. Tears slid off the end of my nose and made mustard-colored splotches in the rosin.

Summer came up behind me. "Here you are," she whispered. "Come on. Big jumps are next. We'll be partners."

She led me to the corner where the students were lining up to dance diagonally across the floor by twos. We leaned against the barre and watched those ahead of us. When Meredith's turn came, Summer whispered, "Look at those terrific jumps!" Then her eyes turned golden. "Course she ain't got no get-up-and-go! Nothing but technique!"

I sighed. *And Peter*, I thought. *She's got Peter, too.*

He was dancing now. He didn't jump very high, but the muscles rippling along his muscular thighs made me tremble. *Oh, Peter, why didn't things work out for us?*

Summer grinned at me. "His jumps aren't bad," she whispered, "except that he can't get off the floor."

I sniffed. "With his body, he doesn't have to jump. Even Mr. Markoff says he'll make a good classical partner, a *danseur noble*, he says."

Peter finished at the far side of the room,

then it was our turn to jump. I gave my holy medal a quick tug and wedged my feet into the opening position. Summer tapped my arm. "This is it, kid!"

Actually, it was a little like jumping double-dutch back at Eastside Elementary. In double-dutch your timing has to be perfect. You have to wait for the two ropes to separate, then you dart through the opening and start jumping.

Here came the music. The ropes parted. Now was the time. Summer and I took off together. I stretched my legs into a full split, sailed, landed without jerking and leaped again.

Suddenly, I was Cynthia Gregory flying through *Don Quixote*. My pilot light flamed. Fire blossomed through my body. I was dancing! Really dancing!

When we finished, Summer and I grinned at each other. Her eyes shimmered. She slapped the palms of her hands against both of mine.

"We did it, girl! We really did it! The super fantastic team of Lara Havas and Summer Jones is on its way. Watch out, New York!"

Chapter 3

"Not bad, Summer and Lara," Mr. Markoff said when we had finished the jumping combination.

"Translated that means we're positively terrific!" Summer whispered. "So why can't he say so?"

"I'm just glad he thinks we did okay," I said. "Also that the audition's over."

Only it wasn't. "All right, everybody, same combination. Other side," Mr. Markoff said.

I groaned. I mean, I was exhausted — and lots of times I get mixed up when I have to reverse steps. But while the pairs in front of us danced, I watched carefully. It looked easy. I took off okay but the light in my chest seemed to have gone out. My legs turned to noodles. My back jerked on every landing. I did a *grand jeté* instead of a *tour jeté*. When I finally managed a *tour jeté* I forgot to allow space for the twisting turn. Wham! My left foot stubbed against one of the pillars. I stood there, dizzy and swaying. I wasn't really hurt. I didn't fall or anything. Maybe if I had been lying unconscious, I wouldn't have heard the other kids tittering or gasping. I wouldn't have felt like such an awful klutz!

Minutes later an arm tightened around my waist. It was Summer's.

"Lord, girl," she whispered, "you take the cake! You aren't hurt, are you?"

Summer had finished the combination and come to lead me to the side of the room. I pressed my face against the barre and started sobbing. Outside the storm howled with me.

Summer patted my shoulder, then rushed back to finish the last combination of the audition.

After class Mr. Markoff and the man from New York joined Stephanie Martin next to the piano. Most of the kids bunched up near the hall door to await the results. Me, I was too embarrassed to move.

Leaning on his cane, Mr. Swensen struggled off the piano bench and hobbled across the room. He has arthritis in his hips even worse than Apa. He waved to us, then tottered off like a three-legged crab. No raincoat. No umbrella. Only the turned-up collar of his old tweed jacket to keep him dry.

Mr. Markoff went over to the students by the door.

"You kids might as well get dressed," he said. "I can see that this discussion is going to take quite a while."

Summer and I looked at each other.

"Why do you suppose?" I asked.

She gave me a trembly smile. "Maybe you and I were so terrific that they're having trouble choosing the runners-up! Come on. We might as well do what he says."

I trailed after her, limping a little on the foot that had bumped the pillar. Ahead of us strolled Peter and Meredith. Their arms circled each other's waists. I hunched my shoulders. As if colliding with the post weren't enough!

They headed into the hall. It leads to the dressing rooms and to a small back studio that used to be the kitchen. They go there to make out. I mean, just the idea knotted my insides! Summer started into the hall after them.

"No!" I cried. "Not that way! Through the foyer to the drinking fountain. I'm thirsty."

She rolled her eyes. "Anything you say, Lara honey."

After the glare in the classroom, the foyer seemed dark. Half the bulbs in the chandelier were burned out. The lightning, flickering in through windows on the staircase and above the front door, only made the foyer seem dimmer between flashes. Water slid off raincoats and umbrellas and into puddles on the floor. The place steamed and smelled of rubber and eucalyptus and old wet wood.

"Lord, look at all the people the storm's drug out," Summer said. "They must be here to get their kids home dry and safe. We're driving you home, Lara."

"We" included Mrs. Martin and Summer. After her family moved from our neighborhood in San José to Oakland, Summer went to live with the Martins so that she could keep on studying at Markoff's. That's when she began calling Mrs. Martin, Stephanie. The rest of us wouldn't dare!

I was waiting behind Summer at the drinking fountain when Peter's mother came swinging through the big double front doors. I forgot all about being thirsty and tried to duck after Summer into the crowd. But Mrs. Hanson headed briskly toward me. Brushing back my hair, I forced a smile. What would I say to her now that Peter and I weren't friends anymore? I needn't have worried. She did all the talking.

"Hello there, Lara. Some storm, isn't it! Can you imagine? The rain was hitting the windshield so fast, the wipers were absolutely useless."

Mrs. Hanson, a school psychologist, is tall and has the same reddish-brown hair as Peter. She had known for a long time that ballet lessons might help his flat feet but she couldn't start him here at Markoff's until after her divorce. Peter's father considers all male dancers sissies. "Or worse," he says. Which is stupid! Lots of them are straight and they're all just about the best athletes in the world!

"Uh, nice to see you, Mrs. Hanson," I said. She glanced beyond me toward the hall.

"Oh, Peter, there you are, darling. Meredith, too. Come here, you two. How did it go?"

I froze. I didn't turn around to look at him but heard him growl, "Okay, I guess. I don't know."

"Peter was simply terrific, Mrs. Hanson," Meredith shrilled. Then with a squeal of laughter, added, "Poor Lara, though, ran into a post."

I hunched my shoulders.

"Oh, too bad! Were you hurt, darling?"

"Just her pride," Meredith gurgled.

"You poor thing." Mrs. Hanson's arm went around me and turned me to face Peter. In the dim room of dark-clad parents, he loomed like a shining young god. His shoulders spread as wide as a football player's. His legs were staunch white pilings. His head with its short clipped brown hair looked small and neat on his massive neck. But his eyes in the darkness seemed shadowy and troubled, not clear and green as I always picture them.

"Just lousy luck about the post," he muttered.

I nodded and stared at the wet floor. If only I could melt into it! Just disappear!

"She'll live," Meredith said, and flipped her wavy blonde hair practically in my face. She rubbed her narrow chin against one of his big swelling biceps and captured his arm in both of hers.

"You'd all better go change out of those

sweaty clothes," Mrs. Hanson said. "And hurry, Peter, the storm's getting worse. Oh, yes, your father phoned."

Peter's head lifted. "What'd he want?"

"He wondered if you'd heard from the colleges you applied to."

"Cripes! What does he expect! It's only January. I won't hear till April."

"I know. And, of course, he had his usual fit when I said you were at ballet. You'd better call him back as soon as you get home, darling. It'll be eleven o'clock there."

Peter's father lives in Washington, D.C., and works at the Pentagon.

"Just wish he'd get off my back," Peter grumbled and, after a quick look at me, let Meredith drag him away.

"Well, see you later, Mrs. Hanson," I said, glad to escape. I was almost at the hall door when I bumped into the tall, big-boned woman who keeps house for Meredith's parents. They're both lawyers and away a lot.

"You! Watch where you're going," she barked at me.

I apologized and tried to hurry on, but she lurched after me and snatched my wrist. Knowing my skin, it would probably turn black and blue where she was clutching me.

"Tell Meredith to get out here right now. Not sit there gabbing."

"All right. Sure," I told the housekeeper while I peered around for Summer. Gone. Then I saw her vanishing into the hall. I rushed after her and into the dressing room.

It was already crowded. If the foyer had seemed gloomy, the dressing room was a dank cellar. Its dark paneled walls are left over from when the room was the library.

Tonight a smelly fog rose from wet raincoats hanging on hooks along the walls and from boots and umbrellas shoved under the benches. I could hardly see myself in the steamed-up mirror.

"You'd think when Mr. Markoff was putting in this dressing room, he could have bought a decent mirror," Meredith said in front of it. She rubbed a space clear. "Even when it's not all steamy, the flaw makes your face look twisted. I wish he'd restore this house the way they're restoring some of the other old Victorians around here."

I dropped onto a bench and shook my hair free of its remaining bobby pins. I let it slide forward over my face, then doubled down to untie my *pointe* shoe ribbons. After that awful meeting with Peter and his mother, not to mention blowing the audition, I wasn't about to discuss restoring old houses, especially not with Meredith.

"Complain, complain," came a voice from the toilet cubicle. "At least we don't have to use the bathroom upstairs anymore. I was always terrified that the wooden tank would spring a leak while I was sitting under it or that the chain would break when I was pulling it to flush the john."

"I know what you mean," Meredith said. "How can those students renting rooms up there stand it?"

"Maybe they're just glad to have a roof over their heads, Meredith honey," Summer said, sitting down beside me. "Besides, it's close to San José State."

Meredith shrugged and squirmed into her designer jeans. She squeezed her belt to the last notch.

"I don't understand why Markoff rents out rooms in the first place. Especially to such a mangy bunch of men. Now if gorgeous Peter gets accepted to San José State next year and moves in upstairs that'll be different, won't it, Lara?"

I bit my lip and worked on my knot. *Creep!*

Rosemary, Meredith's friend, giggled. She was the only one who did. "Chalk one up for Meredith!" Rosemary said.

Beside me Summer muttered, "Talk about snide remarks! Lord, it sounds like the first day we came here. Was it really six years ago?"

Meredith snickered "What a couple of turkeys you two were then! Real dorks! Lara skinny as a beanpole. Fat braids. Huge, scared, smoky-gray eyes. Summer about as big as a mosquito. Teeny quivering braids all over her head."

"And remember how they talked?" Rosemary asked. "Funny peculiar."

"Yeah," Meredith said. "Especially Lara. She still sounded like her parents then. *Dat* instead of *that. Vhat* instead of *what. Vhat ees dat?* Hysterical!"

I gritted my teeth and yanked at my knot. Summer sprang up, slammed her fists on her hips, and set her legs wide apart. She tensed her knees until they bent almost backward.

"Very funny!" she said. "A real stand-up comedian! And, by the way, Meredith honey, your housekeeper's waiting for you, isn't that right, Lara?"

I nodded, lifted my hair off my face, and looked at Meredith. Her head was shrouded by the hand-knit sweater she was dragging over it, but her body stiffened. Good. She deserved to be annoyed.

"Forget her!" Meredith said. "That witch's worse than the last one. Go tell her I'm not leaving until I've heard the verdict."

"Me? Go tell her yourself," Summer said and plopped down beside me again.

"But what's taking them so long to decide?" somebody asked.

"Well, I know what they'll decide about Meredith," Rosemary said. "She's going to New York for sure."

Meredith shook out her wavy blonde mane. "You're undoubtedly right, Rosie, but you never know how things will turn out with auditions, do you, Lara? Or with boys."

My stomach lurched. Meredith was right. I never expected to lose Peter. Of course, when he first started here, he was nothing special — a tall, fairly ordinary-looking boy a year older than I. From the beginning, though, I loved his quick grin, his cheerful "Hey, Lara!" and his green eyes even when they clouded over.

A week or so after he came we began standing next to each other at the barre, the first time by accident. Soon he was coming along to the ice cream parlor with Summer and me. Summer usually had to drive home with Mrs. Martin, so after she left, Peter and I meandered hand in hand to the bus stop. We took different buses, though, because we live on opposite sides of town.

We never really dated, never went to each other's houses, either. He didn't ask me. I didn't ask him. Even if we had, I doubt that my folks would have given their permission. They're old-fashioned. Maybe old-country describes them better. They came to the United States late in 1956 after Apa had fought in the Hungarian Revolution.

"Don't you agree, Lara?" Meredith went on. "You never know how things will turn out?"

I pressed my lips together, unable to answer. *Oh, the creep!*

"Why don't you lay off!" Summer said.

The room became awfully quiet. Outside, the storm roared louder. "Gosh," a girl said, "I wish they'd make up their minds about who's going to the Big Apple."

"Well, for starters, Lara and Summer are," someone said.

"Summer will, all right," Meredith said. She was standing sway-backed in front of the mirror, admiring her own long hair. "She's the shoo-in in the crowd!"

Hands on hips, Summer confronted Meredith. "What's that supposed to mean? Are you saying I'll get a scholarship because I'm black?"

Summer's knees stiffened and she chewed her gum faster. It was our first morning at Markoff's all over again. Only then the argument had begun about Summer's name. "Summer's the name of a season, not a girl!" Meredith had said.

"Yeah? Well, my mama gave me this here name cause that's when I was born. Right in the middle of summer!"

"And your grammar's terrible!" Meredith said.

"Yeah? Well, I don't talk no different than most of the kids at the school me and Lara go to."

At that point five years ago Stephanie Martin had poked her dark head into the dressing room and ended the argument.

The same thing happened now. Just as the argument was getting started, Mrs. Martin opened the door and beckoned to Meredith. Only to Meredith. That really scared me.

"Meredith, you're wanted in Mr. Markoff's office."

Usually Stephanie Martin's phrases flow almost as controlled and mellow as when she sings old Sixties protest songs while chauffeuring us around in her Kharman Ghia. Tonight on the ride over it had been *Double*

27

Damn! Vietnam! But now she bit off her words. "I mean immediately, Meredith!"

Meredith minced across to the door. There she stopped to waggle her narrow behind at us and shake out her pale hair. "Am I the only one?" she asked, smirking.

My stomach twisted. Was she? It sure looked like it! But what also got to me were the words she used. *The only one.*

Right after the phone call came about my brother Steve dying in Vietnam, Apa picked me up out of bed. Tears were probably pouring down his cheeks and soaking into his thick black mustache. All I remember, though, is him rocking me and saying, "You are the only one we have left now, Lara. You're our only little one."

"Well, am I the only one, Mrs. Martin?" Meredith demanded again.

"Just report to Mr. Markoff's office," Stephanie Martin snapped, and left.

"Don't worry, Lara and Summer," a girl said after Meredith pranced out. "You two are the talented ones in our class. You two and Meredith. And maybe also Peter with that divine body of his."

Summer and I didn't look at each other. I gave up on the knot, just ripped the ribbon off my soggy *pointe* shoe and put on T-shirt and jeans. Not designer jeans like Meredith's. No, mine were rejects Mom brings home from the factory where she sews. Beside me on the bench, Summer got dressed, too.

Then even before Meredith came back into the dressing room, we heard her voice out in the hall above the bellowing storm.

"Oh, Peter, isn't it simply marvelous? Just the two of us. Going to New York together!"

Chapter 4

In the dressing room Meredith's words sounded loud as the thunder. "Just the two of us, Peter, going to New York together!"

I slumped on the bench and pressed my chest against my thighs. My sweaty hair flopped forward over my face. I didn't bother to push it back or to look up when Meredith flew in to collect her clothes. I just rubbed my sore foot. I couldn't help seeing her green Adidas flash past, though.

No doubt she was rushing out to meet Peter. I sure hoped the housekeeper whisked Meredith off before she had a chance to kiss him good-night.

The dressing room cleared out fast. Soon only Summer and I remained.

"Well, here we sit like bumps on logs, Mama would say," Summer said. Her voice dragged with tears but she pushed a piece of bubble gum into her mouth and started chewing.

"Shoot, we weren't that bad, were we, Lara?"

I shrugged and sniffed back some left-over tears.

She asked the same question a few minutes later when Stephanie Martin came quietly into the dressing room.

Mrs. Martin leaned against the door and looked down at her feet in their suede pumps. Behind her back, her hands kept twisting the door knob. A shiny lavender raincoat draped across one arm. Her magenta eye shadow and nail polish gleamed under the florescent lamps. So did her eyes. The whites are pure white but the irises are as black as the ebony figurines she and her husband brought back from their honeymoon in Africa. Now the statues decorate their house in Palo Alto.

Mrs. Martin glared at us the way she used to in fifth grade when she found out our class hadn't scored well on some state-wide test or after the principal had popped in unannounced. We called it THE LOOK.

"No," Mrs. Martin said, "you were not that bad. But tonight, unfortunately, you were not that good. Neither were the other students. Except Meredith, of course. Her technique looked very strong. And Peter's body was impressive. I just wish he would work harder. Sometimes I wonder if he takes ballet only to spite his father. But Peter is male and ballet always needs males."

"He's a hunk all right," Summer said, then stuck out her lower lip. "But Meredith? She's nothing but a bunch of muscles and bones and tendons that happen to work good together."

Stephanie Martin's lashes flickered and she smiled slightly. "Work *well* together, sweetheart." She emphasized the first syllable of 'sweetheart.'

"It's called coordination," Mrs. Martin went on, still leaning against the door. "And it is something all good dancers must have."

"Okay, but they also need soul," Summer said. Jumping up and shaking her shoulders, she sang, "And Meredith, she ain't got soul!"

"Kindly spare us the black-face act," Stephanie Martin said. "Just get your things, get rid of the gum, and let's go. Tomorrow we'll discuss the audition. Tonight we're all too tired. Besides, I have to take Lara home. With this storm her mother's no doubt climbing the walls."

I nodded. Right now Mom was probably peering out a spot she had rubbed clear in the steamed-up front window. She would be drying her hands down her apron and muttering to Apa, "I shouldn't of let her go, Frank. I shouldn't of."

Summer grunted and paced the room. "Waiting a couple minutes more isn't going to kill Lara's mother. And I've just got to know why Meredith's going to New York and we aren't. You asked him, didn't you,

Stephanie? The man from New York? What did he say?"

"Not now, Summer," Mrs. Martin snapped. "And get rid of that gum, I told you."

Summer didn't. She faced Stephanie Martin. "I bet I know why you don't want to talk about it, Stephanie. He turned me down because I'm black, didn't he?"

Stephanie Martin's cheeks got hollower. In fifth grade Summer and I used to practice sucking in our cheeks to make them as hollow as Mrs. Martin's.

"That is not the reason, sweetheart!" Mrs. Martin said.

"What is then?"

"And don't you dare use your blackness as a cop-out, Summer Jones. NYBA and its school depend on government grants so they're not likely to discriminate. At least not openly. Mr. Landon turned you down because he thinks you and Meredith are too much alike."

"Oh, give me a break!" Summer wailed.

I stared. "Alike?"

"Wait a minute," Mrs. Martin said. "Just back up and let me finish. Mr. Landon said Summer and Meredith are the same kind of dancer. *Allegro* dancers. And because he thinks Meredith's technique is better, he chose her."

Summer stood with hands on hips, feet apart. She chomped her gum. "Do you really believe that garbage, Stephanie? That he chose her because he thinks her technique is better?"

"I believe he thinks so."

"And what about Lara with her high extensions and stretched-out *penchés*?" Summer continued. "Lara's certainly not like Meredith. What's his excuse about Lara?"

Stephanie Martin sighed. Her shoulders even drooped a little. She slid her fingers along the bench, to make sure, I guess, that it wouldn't get her dress wet or dirty. She sat down.

"I think you have the talent to become a lovely dancer someday, Lara, but right now I have to agree with Mr. Landon. He said your dancing isn't strong enough, that you lack concentration and are a little too tall for ballet."

I took a sharp breath. Tears stung my eyes.

"More bull," Summer said, pacing again. "Lara just had the jitters tonight. She's as strong as anybody when she's with it. And being tall is what gives her the gorgeous lines."

"I know that," Mrs. Martin said. "But being tall also makes her different from most ballet dancers. Just as being black makes you different."

Summer glowered. "But it's okay to be different. That's what you keep saying. Remember our first day in fifth grade? You made me write on the board twenty-five times, IT'S OKAY TO BE DIFFERENT. IT'S OKAY TO BE DIFFERENT, all because I asked Lara, 'How's the weather up there?' Boy, did my hand get sore!"

Summer grinned at me. I remembered all right. Over that vacation I had grown four whole inches and was almost as tall as I am now. And here came this little pipsqueak fresh from North Carolina to tease me!

"Being different is fine," Mrs. Martin said, "but it makes competing all the harder."

"But Cynthia Gregory is tall," I said, "and she's a ballerina with American Ballet Theatre, so I thought being tall was okay. Was that why you didn't dance professionally, Mrs. Martin? Because you were too tall?"

Summer grinned at Mrs. Martin. "She never got into a ballet company because she's black."

"Enough!" Stephanie Martin snapped. "My training was interrupted when I was about Summer's age. Fifteen. So when —"

"That's when you up and ran off with that guitar player, wasn't it?" Summer interrupted. "With Blackbird."

Mrs. Martin glanced at Summer and away. My mouth dropped open. "Blackbird?" I asked.

"Blackbird was not his name," Mrs. Martin said.

"What was then?" Summer asked.

"Never mind."

"Guess I'll just have to ask Daniel."

Daniel is Stephanie Martin's husband, a computer engineer.

Mrs. Martin aimed THE LOOK at Summer. "When I took up my training again, it was too late. My technique never returned to its former level, never became what it should have been."

"But what happened to Blackbird?" Summer asked.

"I thought you wanted to talk about the audition and your future as a dancer, sweetheart."

Summer poked out her lower lip. "I guess."

"All right then. So besides being tall and black, I wasn't good technically. At least not good enough."

"But what is good enough?" Summer asked.

I nodded. With both hands I combed my hair back from my face. "I always thought you believed we were good enough, Mrs. Martin. I mean, the way you collected money from the teachers at Eastside so we could start taking ballet here."

"Yeah," Summer said, "if we aren't good enough, how come you did that? And how come NYBA pays our tuition here every year?"

"You are both confusing your potential talent with realized technical achievement," Stephanie Martin said.

"How about translating that?" Summer asked, grinning. "You know, put it into Standard English."

I snickered but stopped when I saw the uptight look on Mrs. Martin's face.

"Tonight," Stephanie Martin said, cutting each word off short, "tonight is what we are talking about. Tonight you were not invited to the final audition. Either of you. And you want to know why. Very well, maybe now is the time for a little reality therapy, after all. Let's take a good hard look at the way things really are in this world."

I sighed. Summer groaned out loud. We knew all about Mrs. Martin's reality sessions from fifth grade and from when we had her for intermediate ballet classes.

"Borrring!" Summer said.

"Be quiet and listen," Mrs. Martin said. "Lara, you are at least three inches taller than the average female ballet dancer. Summer, you are black. And, at present, there seem to be very few openings for ballet dancers who are tall or for ballet dancers who are black."

"Or for tall black dancers who run off with guitar —" Summer began, but shut up when Mrs. Martin gave her THE LOOK.

"As I was saying, you both are going to have to be better than simply good enough. You're going to have to be two or three times better than a technically proficient, short, blonde dancer like Meredith Shafer. You will have a hard time getting into a *corps de ballet* in which the average dancer is five feet three and white. You'll have to be soloists at least. Better yet, principal dancers."

"Like Cynthia Gregory," I said.

"Yes. And like Virginia Johnson with

Dance Theater of Harlem."

"But there are black dancers in *corps*, too," Summer said.

"How many?" Mrs. Martin asked.

"Well, there's at least one at ABT. And maybe a couple in the San Francisco Ballet. Then in the Harlem company everybody's black."

"All right, Summer, you're good at math. Figure it out. How many does that add up to throughout the entire country?"

Summer slumped. "I see what you mean."

I sighed. "Me, too."

Then Summer grinned. "So what it adds up to," she said, snapping her fingers, going into her song and dance act again, "what it adds up to is that we're going to have to be simply terrific. Sue-oo-per, doo-oo-per fantastic! And wc will be. We will!"

I couldn't help cheering up a little. Even Mrs. Martin smiled.

"Good!" she said. "And I'm going to see that you are. I'm going to work both of you harder than ever before. So that next time there's an audition you'll make it."

"Next time?" Summer asked.

"Why yes, sweetheart, next time. Being turned down once isn't the end of the world, you know. Though with this storm and your long faces I'm beginning to wonder if tonight isn't maybe Doomsday or the Deluge or something. Now, for the last time, get rid of that gum, Summer. Then let's get out of here while we still can."

Chapter 5

Stephanie Martin might not think failing the audition was the end of the world, but that's how it seemed to me.

"Put on your raincoats," Mrs. Martin said. "It's terrible outside. The radio says Highway 17 to Santa Cruz is closed at the summit. Creeks are overflowing, including Coyote. So is the Guadalupe River between here and your house, Lara. We've got to get going."

I pulled on the rubber boots Mom made me wear and my awful yellow slicker. I tried not to notice Summer putting on her silky brown trench coat. She hasn't had it long. Only since her braces came off. The coat's a gift from Stephanie Martin.

We followed Mrs. Martin into the foyer. Except for the three of us, it was empty. The whole house was empty. The dancers were gone. The college students, who rented the rooms upstairs, hadn't returned from the holidays. Even the man from New York and

Mr. Markoff had taken off for Mr. Markoff's apartment.

Mrs. Martin opened one of the double front doors. Rain slanted in. Beyond the short patch of lawn the street was a river, a dark monster roaring and swirling along in the shine of street lamps and in flashes of lightning. It was as scary as some of the Hungarian fairy tales Apa used to tell me.

"Water from curb to curb," Mrs. Martin said, "and beginning to spill onto the front sidewalk. The creek at the end of the street must be overflowing. If this keeps up, the house will flood. Let's go."

She and Summer stepped onto the slippery wooden porch, but I huddled in the doorway.

"Come on, Lara," Mrs. Martin called. "You won't melt."

I pushed my icy hands into the cold, stiff pockets of my slicker. "It looks so awful out there," I said.

Were Mom and Apa this terrified on the stormy night they left Hungary? On his back Apa carried three-year-old Steve in a knapsack through miles of drenched fields.

Behind us in the foyer now the phone began ringing. I jumped at the hollow sound. "Good grief, who's that?"

"Probably some parent wondering where her child is," Mrs. Martin said in the doorway. "Let it ring. We can't take time to answer it."

"But I know — I just know it's my folks." I ran back to the office under the stairs and picked up the receiver. It was Apa. I pictured him leaning his painful hip against the old metal kitchen counter and clamping the receiver to his ear. His huge walrus mustache would be curling down over the mouthpiece.

"Here's Lara," I heard him yell to Mom in Hungarian. That showed how worried he was. My family hasn't spoken much Hungarian since way before I was born. My brother's kindergarten teacher said speaking it at home was keeping Steve from learning English.

"No school teacher is going to make me give up my own language," Apa said. He still argues with Mom in Hungarian and swears in it. I understand a little but wish I could really speak it. Then we would have our own private language. Sort of like Summer does.

Over the phone now I heard Mom yelling in the background. She likes me to call her Mom, not Anya, the Hungarian word for mother. But like Apa tonight she was speaking Hungarian. "My saints! Don't hang up. Let me talk to her."

I could hear her scuttling over the linoleum that near the kitchen door is worn down to the black. Below her headscarf, her thick gray braid would be bouncing against her dark baggy sweater.

She came on the telephone, shouting. But she wasn't shouting only to be heard above the thunder. Mom always shouts on the phone, thunder or no thunder.

"You tell that Mrs. Martin to get you right home, dear heart," Mom said, then hung right up. She hates talking on the phone, but at least they knew I was okay and I knew the same about them.

I went out on the porch again just as the lights died along the block. The ones in the foyer behind us blinked out, too. A gust of wind shot rain straight into our faces. I backed inside. So did Summer and Mrs. Martin.

"I'm going to phone Daniel," she said. "He'll know precisely what the road conditions are all over Santa Clara county and the very safest route to Lara's house and to Palo Alto. He's worked with computers so long, he thinks like one."

She disappeared into the office under the stairs. Summer and I clung together in the doorway. The only light came from flashes of lightning through the window on the staircase and through the transom above the front door.

"Maybe we'll be marooned," Summer said, giggling nervously. "Like people on TV. Maybe TV camera men'll come take our pictures."

"Yeah," I said, "maybe we'll be on the eleven o'clock news."

But I was shivering too much to really care. All I wanted was to get home.

Through the darkness I heard Mrs. Martin's voice — clear, sharp, a little breathless, too. "I can't phone out. Not even a dial tone. The thing's dead."

The way her voice shook I knew she was really worried. So I got really worried, too.

"We'll have to take our chances," she said. "The Kharman Ghia's awfully small and low to the ground but if the water's not too high maybe we can get through."

She opened the front door, then quickly slammed it. "Not this way! The water's nearly up on the porch. Let's try the back. The ground's higher there. Besides, that's where my car's parked."

Summer and I groped after her through the dark hallway, past the dressing rooms and into the small studio where Peter and Meredith spend a lot of time these days. I hunched my shoulders. The rain pounded louder than ever on the room's flat roof.

Mrs. Martin muttered a swear word then said, "The key doesn't fit. I'll have to use the front door after all. So it's back to the foyer."

Her heels clicked away, went far ahead of me. Darkness swirled against my eyes, pressed in on them. My folks and little Steve must have felt scared like this hiding in dark barns and under railroad trestles on their way to the Austrian-Hungarian border.

"Lara? Where are you, girl?" Summer called. Her voice was shrill.

Mine shook. "Here."

She took my hand. Hers was even colder. We stumbled along until I saw a gray half circle and a gray rectangle. The windows in the foyer.

"Water's coming under the front door now," Mrs. Martin said. "It's rising faster than I thought. Here, Summer, take my shoes. Put them on Mr. Markoff's desk. Or there'll go a hundred and fifty dollars down the drain. I'll wade around to get the car."

"You can't go out there!" Summer said.

"You'll be washed away," I said. I didn't add, "And drowned!" But I thought it.

I reached into the front of my slicker and grasped my medal.

Mrs. Martin pulled open the front door and left. Water poured in, was suddenly up to my ankles. Now I was glad that Mom had made me wear these boots.

"We've got to shut the door," Summer said.

I helped her close it but water poured underneath.

"Maybe we could sit on the steps," I said, shivering.

"Good idea," Summer said.

We were wading toward the staircase when an explosion jolted the house. We grabbed hold of each other. Her heart thudded, her breath caught. Or was it my own heart and my own breath?

"Lord, what was that?" Summer cried. "It came from the back of the house."

"Good grief, that's where Mrs. Martin went," I said.

"Come on," Summer said. "Let's try to get

out a window. Break one, if we have to. We've got to find Stephanie."

Summer grabbed my hand, pulled me along the dark hallway again. The rain got louder. We must be back in the flat-roofed studio. This time though, wind and rain blasted straight into my face. I stumbled into something huge, wet, prickly. I let out a scream. I screamed on and on. Summer started shaking me. My head bobbed back and forth, back and forth. My teeth snapped against each other.

"Stop it, Lara. Get hold of yourself. It's only a big old eucalyptus branch."

Yes, now I smelled its sharp, cold odor. Like the medicine Mom rubs on my chest when I get a cold.

"Must have crashed right through the roof," Summer went on. She sounded out of breath. As if she had just done *tours jetés* across the room. "So we can't get out. Not this way. We've got to go back and see if Stephanie's okay."

Summer pulled me along. Inside my stiff cold slicker, I was stiff and cold. I couldn't even scream anymore. And it was so dark. Then out of the darkness came Mrs. Martin's voice. "Lara. Summer. Where are you?"

"Here. Right here," Summer said. We were back in the flooded foyer.

"Thank God!" Mrs. Martin's arms went around us. Her heart thumped against mine. She could hardly talk.

"A branch, a huge one, crushed the car. Another second and I'd have been inside. So now we'll have to stay. Come on."

"Where?" Summer asked.

"Upstairs," Mrs. Martin said.

"Upstairs?" That was Summer's shaky voice. "Terrific! Haven't been upstairs since the college students moved in. What with you and Mr. M. being so uptight and making the second floor out of bounds. But do you think the TV camera men can find us up there and take our pictures for the eleven o'clock news?"

"Stop that nonsense, Summer," Mrs. Martin snapped. "Just get upstairs. Lara, why are you standing there?"

I felt her pushing me through the water and darkness and up the stairs. Then somebody grabbed my arm and dragged me down to sit on the steps.

"Lara and I are staying right here by the window," Summer said. "We aren't budging till we spot the TV men."

A minute later she let out a whoop. "There they are, driving in from the back alley. The TV men. See the headlights?"

I looked out. Lighting up the gray slashes of rain were two long, blue-white tubes of brightness. Headlights, for sure!

Boots tramped along the side porch to the front. A fist banged the door. "Stephanie!" a voice yelled. "Are you in there, Stephanie? Open up."

"Shoot, it's only Daniel," Summer said.

Her giggle quavered. "Heck, no TV men."

She took off down the stairs. I couldn't follow her. My numb legs wouldn't unbend. My hands seemed glued to the banister. In the darkness Mrs. Martin pried them free and guided me down the stairs.

The front door swung open and in came a beam of strong light. It raked around until it picked out Mrs. Martin.

"Thank God, you're safe, Stephanie," Mr. Martin said, pulling her against his chest. "It's raining cats and dogs out there."

"More like tigers and timber wolves, wouldn't you say?" Mrs. Martin asked dryly. "Come on, Daniel. We have to get the girls out of here."

He let her go and beamed the light on Summer and me. "All right. No time to waste. Just follow instructions, everybody. I'll get you all home safe and sound. You first, Summer," he said.

With her in his arms, he ducked into the storm. Minutes later he was back for me.

"Do you really think the truck'll make it to my house, Mr. Martin?" I asked.

"We're not going there tonight, Lara. It's out of the question. Too risky. It'll be difficult enough getting up to Palo Alto."

"But I've got to go home," I said. "My folks'll think I've drowned or something."

"You can phone them from our house. Now put your arms around my neck and I'll carry you out to the truck."

I started to back away. I mean, I'm five

eight and weigh about a hundred and fifteen. That's why I hate *pas de deux* class these days. Peter's the only one tall enough to partner me. I have to dance with him even though he's going with Meredith now. It's so embarrassing.

Mr. Martin picked me up as if I were a three-year-old and marched with me around the flooded porch to the back. There his truck waited with its motor rumbling. Its headlights gleamed into the slanting streaks of rain.

He slid me along the front seat and up against Summer. A minute later he settled Mrs. Martin next to me. Her satiny raincoat caressed my hand. She smelled faintly of vanilla. She slipped an arm along the back rest behind me. I leaned against her carefully so she wouldn't notice. At Eastside Elementary when teachers have yard duty they usually let you walk along beside them. Mrs. Martin never would. She believes a teacher can't teach effectively if she gets too friendly with her pupils.

"Wait, Daniel," Mrs. Martin called. "Would you get my shoes? The suede pumps. I left them on the desk."

He paused in the beam of the headlights. He had on a navy blue trench coat. Summer claims all his clothes are navy blue. Even his pj's.

"Be sensible, Stephanie! Why were you wearing pumps on a night like this, anyway? I'm not going to waste precious minutes hunting around for them at this point in time."

"Then I'll get them," she said, and tried to open the truck door. Daniel held it shut.

"No. Stay put. We're leaving as soon as I check to be sure the front door is locked. We don't want any looters breaking in."

"Looters?" Summer muttered. "They'd have to be crazy to be out on a night like this."

Seconds later Mr. Martin was back and slid in behind the steering wheel. "Fasten your seatbelts, ladies," he ordered.

Shivering between Summer and Mrs. Martin, I buckled the ends of mine together. Rain drummed on the metal roof. With the eerie whiteness of an atomic explosion, lightning glared off the faces of Summer and the Martins.

I shuddered. Was this the same night that Meredith and Peter won and Summer and I lost chances to go to New York? It seemed so long ago. Now all that mattered was this storm and getting home.

Chapter 6

The ride to Palo Alto seemed to take forever. Driving up Bayshore Highway was like plowing up the Sacramento River in one of those landing craft I've seen on TV, the kind that go on both land and water. They were used mostly in World War II but also in Vietnam where Steve died.

I sighed. Poor Steve. Why did he have to go and get killed? When I asked Apa that once, he frowned. His scrubby black brows folded down over his eyes. His accent got thicker.

"Why did Steve get killed, little one? Who knows. In Hungary most of my friends died to try to free their country from the Communists. I was willing to die for that, too, but when danger threatened Steve and your mother I had to get them out."

Apa shook his bald head and sighed. "About Steve in Vietnam, I wish I knew. He went because he was sent. Died for the same reason. I'd rest easier if I knew his dying was for a good purpose."

I ducked my shoulders and stared out at the storm.

Summer poked me. "Lara, I'm talking to you, girl. Look how hard the rain's coming down."

I nodded. Through half circles cleared by the windshield wipers, I saw gray lines of rain blowing now this way, now that, like a heavy beaded curtain.

"By the by, Stephanie," Mr. Martin said suddenly, "where did you leave the Ghia? In a safe place, I hope."

I caught my breath and heard Summer catch hers. The wipers kept whack-whacking. I thought of Stephanie Martin's little car crushed under the giant eucalyptus branch.

"I'm sure it's perfectly safe," Mrs. Martin said coolly. "Nobody's going to steal it tonight."

A giggle spurted from Summer. One nearly choked me.

We reached the Martins' house just before midnight. Water gushed along their street but wasn't over the curbs yet. Daniel Martin put the truck in the garage while Summer and I followed Stephanie Martin toward the house.

"Walk under the eaves," she said. "That way you'll stay dry. Daniel will be in after he finishes doing whatever he does to that precious truck of his."

She unlocked the door and led us through

a roofless garden room. The Atrium, she calls it. Always before, when I've come here with Summer or to school parties, the plants have been bright green and shining in the sunlight.

Tonight the Atrium streamed with water. Camellias and fuchsias huddled dark and dripping in the downpour. The fountain overflowed. Everything was drenched, cold, abandoned. That's how I felt, too. Also a little homesick. I thought of Apa sitting with a book or newspaper, resting after cleaning houses all day. His feet in red felt slippers would be reaching toward the orange glow of the gas heater, his shiny bald dome resting on the fake leather of Old Magyar. That's what we call his ancient reclining chair. Magyar is the Hungarian name for Hungary and the people who first settled there. I had to phone home right away.

"Come on, Lara," Summer called. "It's freezing out here."

She pulled me into the warm entry hall. One of the ebony statues the Martins had brought back from Africa grinned at us. "Hi, Kunta Kinte," Summer said. "You keeping dry, old man?"

I giggled, mostly because it was so good to be warm and safe.

"Let's go to my room, Lara," Summer said.

But Mrs. Martin was brisk. "No. Take off your rain things here. I'll get us something to eat while you two take hot showers. And to save time, Summer, let Lara use your bathroom while you go around to ours. Lara, I'll put out one of my nightgowns. We're about the same size."

I stood in the hallway, fidgeting with my hair.

"What is it, Lara? Speak up," Mrs. Martin said.

"I just wondered if I could call my folks first."

"Certainly. Use the phone in the kitchen. I hope they'll understand why we couldn't bring you home tonight."

"Oh, me, too." If Mom didn't understand, no telling what she might do. She might even use it as an excuse not to let me take ballet anymore.

"Come along, Summer," Mrs. Martin said, "I'm sure Lara can manage a phone call without your assistance."

When they left, I went into the kitchen. The phone hangs on the wall opposite a broad-shouldered gray-green refrigerator-freezer that's almost as big as our entire kitchen.

I dialed, but got a busy signal. Did that mean the storm had taken out the phones where I live? Or was Mom, guessing I was here, trying to call me? I waited and tried again. Then again. Every time, the same busy signal.

"Well, did you get through to your parents, Lara?" Mrs. Martin asked, coming back to the kitchen.

"No. I guess our phone's out of order."

"We'll try again in the morning. Now stop worrying and go take your shower."

I went down the hall to the bathroom. Its daffodil-yellow fixtures and tiles looked so cheerful and warm that I started to relax. At home our bathroom is drab, with a rust-stained bathtub and a toilet you have to flush with a bucket of water.

I sat down on the little chair upholstered in yellow velvet and pulled off my clothes. On a hook near the dressing table, Mrs. Martin had hung her creamy silk nightgown. Sexy! I slithered into it after my shower and felt sexy, too. Willowy instead of gangling. If only Peter could see me now, good-bye Meredith!

A silk robe went with the gown. I put it on and headed for the kitchen.

"Don't stand there in the doorway, Lara," Mrs. Martin said. "Come sit down. There are toasted cheese sandwiches and hot chocolate."

"Yeah," Summer said. Her eyes gleamed at me. "You can sit by me if you're shy of Daniel."

Blushing, I peeked at him from between curtains of hair that swooped forward over my cheeks. He was wearing navy blue, just as Summer had predicted, but navy blue sweats, not pj's. His spine was as straight as the back of his chair.

"You'll get used to Daniel," Summer went on. "Actually, he's kind of sweet when he lightens up a little."

"Let Daniel alone and eat your supper,"

Mrs. Martin said. "Then I want you and Lara to go to bed and right to sleep. This is not to be a slumber party."

Summer stood up and pushed in her chair. "After everything that's happened, I'm not very hungry. Guess I'll turn in right now."

"Not until you finish your supper," Mr. Martin said. "You can't have eaten since lunch so you need to eat at this point in time."

I stared at him. Would he insist that I clean up my plate, too, like Mom does? The toast looked greasy with soaked-in butter, and the chocolate grayish with too much milk.

"For heaven's sake, Daniel, let Summer go to bed," Mrs. Martin said. "Let them both go. They won't starve before morning."

Summer went off and I was glad to follow.

"Is he always that picky?" I asked when we got to her room.

"Picky's the word," Summer said. "Always complaining about stupid little things like the toast getting burned or his socks getting lost in the wash. Borrring! That's what Daniel is. How can she stand him after Blackbird?"

Summer slid into the lower bunk. With Mrs. Martin's nightgown clinging to my legs, I climbed to the upper. Careful not to trip, I pretended I was Cynthia Gregory slinking through her Siren role in *The Prodigal Son*.

"Do you think she's still in love with Blackbird?" I asked after I wriggled between the fresh, cotton sheets.

Summer snorted. "How should I know? Lord, you're so romantic, Lara! I can't believe the way you moon over Peter!"

"Wait till you fall in love," I snapped.

Neither of us said anything more. After awhile I heard her sniffling. Maybe she was coming down with a cold. Or was she crying because she hadn't won a scholarship to New York?

"Summer?" I whispered, feeling sorry I had snapped at her.

"What?"

"Well, are you okay?"

"Okay? I've let her zap away everything I was before, including how I talked, the real me. She even got rid of my family. And for what? I didn't even make the first audition."

"Maybe it'll work out," I said.

Silence.

The rain poured off the eaves. In the darkness I pressed my hands along my body. My thighs and belly felt silky and firm. What would it be like to be lying here with Peter?

When I woke up the sun was slanting in through the sliding glass doors and making a bright rectangle across the carpet. Water gargled down a rain gutter on the patio outside Summer's room. The rain itself had stopped.

For a minute I felt at peace, happy just to be lying here. Except for the gargling, the only sounds were the cracklings and snappings of the all-wooden house. Ours is much older and crackles even louder. Then I remembered the audition and Peter and Meredith. Also my folks at home not knowing where I was.

Since Summer wasn't in the room, it was probably late. I slid down the ladder and found my clothes neatly folded on her dresser. Sometime between midnight and now Mrs. Martin must have washed them and run them through the dryer. Imagine having a dryer! Mom hangs our clothes on sagging lines in the backyard.

I put on my jeans and T-shirt and went down the hall to look for Summer. The Martins' house is beautiful, all glass and redwood. It was built in the early sixties by a company called Eichler. I looked in the huge living room with its long glass wall that opens onto a deck and swimming pool. Summer wasn't in the living room or the family room, either.

The family room, with a special springy floor for dancing, is bare except for a ballet barre on one wall and, across from it, a big mirror. Summer is really lucky to have this room to practice in.

I found her in the kitchen not looking lucky at all. Chin in hand, elbow on the table, she stared at the green formica top.

"What's wrong?" I asked.

Before Summer could answer, Mrs. Martin came in. She looked tired and kind of old. For the first time I noticed tiny lines radiating from her eyes. She's thirty-four.

"Well, there you are, sleepyhead," she said to me. "Summer's having her breakfast. Would you like an egg?"

"No, thank you. Just cereal. But first I'd like to phone my folks, if that's okay."

"I've already tried, Lara, and couldn't reach them. The phone company says the telephones in your area are still out. Summer, I did talk to your mother in Oakland, though. Your stepfather had already left for the docks. She and the kids are fine except for Damone. He has his usual I-hate-to-go-to-school stomachache. I suspect yours is the same kind."

"I told you before, I don't have a stomachache, Stephanie," Summer said, sticking out her lower lip. "I just don't see why I have to go to school after everything that happened yesterday. It's already ten o'clock. So by the time I got there I'd have only one class left. Besides, Lara's here."

"Not for long," Mrs. Martin said. "I took Daniel to work so I could have the truck. I'll drop you off at Paly before I drive Lara home. I don't want you to miss that quiz you have in French today. You want to make the honor list as usual, don't you?"

"I guess."

"So, you're to go to French, Summer, then return here to practice. No dawdling, remember. I'll be back in time to drive you over to Markoff's this afternoon to practice. Then to take my intermediate class."

Summer sprang up. "Intermediate class?"

"Yes. Starting today, if the studio can be used after last night's storm, you're to take it as well as the advanced class. And, Lara, I'd like you there at least by three."

I sighed. "Four o'clock is the earliest I can make it. You know how Mom is about school. I wish she'd let me go half day the way Summer does."

"Stephanie," Summer demanded, "what's all this garbage about taking intermediate class, plus our regular class, plus extra practicing? Trying to work us to death or something?"

Mrs. Martin examined her magenta fingernails. "If you want to go to New York, you have to work."

"Far as I know," Summer said, "since we blew the audition last night, New York is out of the question."

"Whether it is or not, you both must be prepared to take any opportunity that presents itself."

Summer sputtered. "Stephanie, do you know something we don't?"

Mrs. Martin shrugged. "That's all I'm going to say right now. So finish your breakfasts and let's get going."

Chapter 7

"Now what was that double-talk about going to New York, Stephanie?" Summer asked. She leaned forward and looked across me at Mrs. Martin. We were all in the truck on our way to Summer's school. "At breakfast you sounded as if you had something up your sleeve."

"Not me. I was speaking in glittering generalities, sweetheart. I want you prepared for any opportunity that presents itself."

"Oh." Summer slumped against the seat. So did I. I was tired after yesterday. Also discouraged. I stared out the windshield, barely aware of the branches and leaves the truck was dodging around. There were shingles, too. Storm debris lay along the streets like driftwood washed ashore by the ocean.

We passed a boy on a bicycle. He snatched off his cap, waved it, then reared up onto the back wheel and did some really wobbly "wheelies."

"Who's that?" I asked.

"John." Summer sounded as if she couldn't care less.

"Who's John? He's sure putting on a show. Is he somebody special?"

"Just some boy or other."

"Well, he's certainly been hanging around a lot for being 'just some boy or other'," Mrs. Martin said.

"So he likes me," Summer said. "But he's boring. All he talks about are stupid bicycles."

He must not be important, I decided. She had never mentioned him before. And if she liked him, she wouldn't care what he talked about. Like I don't — didn't — when Peter went on about curling barbells and reps and sets. His eyes got shiny green like ocean breakers with the sun gleaming through them. "Hey, Lara, feel this!" he would tell me, and flex his arms so I could press his hard, rubbery biceps. "Seventeen inches!" he said. But once in a while he would mention his dad. Then his eyes went vague.

"My father thinks Mom is too permissive, is ruining me, raising me to be able to be nothing but a garbage man," Peter had said once when we were walking to the bus stop. "That's what they fought about, among other things, before they got divorced. Still do. He wanted me to go to West Point and study engineering like he did. She said he was trying to relive his life through me. But it turned out my grades were so bad, he gave up on West Point."

"My folks argue about me, too, Peter. Mostly about ballet."

"Hey, you should hear my dad on that subject. He was in both Korea and Nam and thinks only the Army will ever make a man of me."

I sighed. As if Peter wasn't one already! He was sure all the man I wanted! And Meredith had him.

Summer poked me. "I said, we're here, Lara. This is Paly. Famous Palo Alto High School. Da-DAH!"

We bumped up a wide driveway and headed along an asphalt road between clumps of dusty evergreens. I had never been here before. It has lots of straggly old pine trees. And a bell tower and red-tiled roofs. Everything is sure different from St. Catherine's.

No scratchy green-and-black uniforms, for one thing. But the biggest difference is boys! Paly has them. St. Catherine's doesn't. A good reason, plus high academic standards, for me to go there after eight years in public school, my parents thought. They decided it was worth some of the money from Steve's insurance and from what they had saved, penny by penny, for Steve to go to college. But he never used it. Instead he was drafted.

"Drop me by the flagpole," Summer said. Mrs. Martin did, and from the curb Summer called, "See y'all."

Half an hour later Mrs. Martin let me off at my house. Apa waved from our front porch. But Mom, wiping her hands on her apron, came thumping down the wooden steps. When she clapped me against her bosom, her sharp chin dug into my shoulder.

"Thank the Blessed Virgin you're home, dear heart!" Then she pushed me out to arms' length and frowned. "But where you been all the night long?"

Her eyes were red-rimmed and swollen. Her skin, in contrast to her red-and-purple head scarf, was the pasty color of dough before it's baked. She grabbed me to her breast again.

"I should never of let you go. So worried we was. The phone broke so we couldn't call Mrs. Martin or the police or nobody. And the roads was too flooded to go looking for you in the van. You're the only, only one we got left, dear heart."

Tears spilled down both sides of her nose but, when she saw Mrs. Martin at the truck window, Mom scrubbed at her eyes with the hem of her apron.

"Sorry, we couldn't bring Lara home last night," Mrs. Martin called. "It wasn't safe. Right now, I have to go find out if my car can be salvaged. See you in class this afternoon, Lara."

I hoped so, but the way Mom's pale lips clamped together when Mrs. Martin mentioned class, I'd be lucky ever to go to ballet again.

"Humph!" Mom muttered so that only I could hear. "She hardly gets you home, then talks about you leaving again." Mom smiled and waved at Mrs. Martin, though, then herded me up the stairs.

Apa had backed partway down and was clinging to the wobbly railing. With all the rain last night, his arthritis must really be hurting. Not enough to make him bring out his cane, however. He would rather suffer than use one like Mr. Swensen does.

Apa didn't say anything. He just balanced on a narrow wooden step and hugged and hugged me. He was wearing work clothes — blue jeans, an old blue sweater Mom knit years ago, and a black beret over his baldness. But, to me, he looked distinguished, like a baron from one of the folktales he used to tell me. In Hungary, although he worked in a factory, he took classes at the university and wrote poetry.

"I was afraid you'd be off cleaning houses, Apa," I said when he released me. For the first time I noticed a few coarse strands of white in the thick black of his eyebrows and mustache.

"How could I until you came home, little one?" he said. Although he talks with an accent, Apa has a poet's ear for language and speaks English almost as perfectly as Mrs. Martin. He patted my cheek.

"Do you have the day off, too, Mom?" I asked, following her up the steps.

She nodded. "I would of taken it anyway but this morning the boss drops by and says the factory basement's flooded. 'Don't come in this week,' he says. I guess he figures to save money by not having to pay us."

"It sounds to me as if he's losing money by not getting his jeans made," Apa muttered. He used the railing to pull himself up the stairs.

"That's all you know about it, Frank. Not a practical bone in your body. How come you're still home? It's your day to clean Mrs. Johnson's house."

"Listen, old woman, I'll go when I'm ready. Mrs. Johnson's dirty house will wait."

"My saints! Don't we sound grand this morning! Maybe I should call you 'Your Lordship.' Better get a move on, Your Lordship, before Mrs. Johnson decides she don't like streaky windows and fires you like all the others done. GM, too."

"GM did not fire me. I was laid off."

I shook my head but couldn't help laughing. My folks are like the sparrows in the straggly Chinese elm near our front steps. Suddenly they're squabbling and flying at each other. Then just as suddenly they stop.

"Laid off. Fired. What's the difference?" Mom asked. "Come on, Lara. I'll fix you something to eat. Also I got things to say to you."

I sighed. She was sure to begin on ballet.

But Mom took only two steps across the porch before she halted and scowled down at the floor. "Hear that, old man? Hear that creaking? That board's been loose ever since we moved here."

"Don't tell me. Tell the landlord!"

Mom grunted. "Him? He never fixes nothing! Not since we come here thirty years ago. So since you're hanging round this morning, get a hammer. Or is Your Lordship going to sit and read the newspaper all day?"

"Yes. We're taking things easy for a while, Old Magyar and I." Apa limped into the front room, clutched the back of his chair, and lowered himself onto its sagging Naugahyde seat.

Old Magyar, this house, even Apa's job at GM came through the efforts of a certain Mrs. Laura Neal Reilly, who back in the Fifties headed the Refugee Committee of our church. To show our family's appreciation for Mrs. Reilly, Mom wanted to name me after her. Apa, however, insisted that I have a good Hungarian name. Mom got around him by claiming she was giving me his mother's name. Klara with the 'k' dropped off becomes Lara.

"You plan to loll here all day, Frank?" Mom asked now.

"Listen, old woman, I'm tired. I didn't sleep well last night, what with Lara not home and you muttering to the Holy Virgin till rosy dawn."

"Blasphemer! It's a mortal sin to talk like that, Frank."

"And don't call me Frank. My name is Ferenc."

I sighed. The name game! One of their favorites.

"Not in America your name ain't Ferenc," Mom said. "You was Frank at GM. Frank in the phone book now. Frank's All-American Housekeeping Service."

"You were the one who put that in the yellow pages. You were the one who changed István's name to plain Steve, too."

Mom stopped in the kitchen doorway. "My saints! That was ages ago, Frank. His kindergarten teacher said it wasn't healthy for such a shy little fellow to have such a strange name."

I covered my ears. Suddenly their quarreling wasn't funny anymore. "Enough is enough," I cried. "István. Steve. What does it matter? He's dead!"

They both stared at me. I was shaking all over. The audition, I guess, plus the storm last night and everything else had gotten to me.

"It matters," Apa said quietly, picking up his newspaper. "It helps me to think of him as István, the name of Hungary's patron saint. A brave, proud name."

"Sorry, Apa. Sorry, Mom," I said, frowning, flipping my hair out of my eyes.

"Well, I guess you're just plain worn out, dear heart," Mom said. "Hungry, too. Come out to the kitchen and I'll get you something warm and filling. You're way too skinny these days. All this dancing!"

I hunched my shoulders. "I ate at Mrs. Martin's, Mom."

"Humph! A sliver of bread. A thimbleful of orange juice. That woman's skinny, too."

I followed Mom into the kitchen but looked

back at Apa. He sent me a quick wink. "Your mother didn't sleep any better than I did," he called. "So do what she says, little one, or no telling what will happen."

Mom grunted and pointed toward the table. I sat down. Now she would bring up ballet. I wrapped my long legs around the chair legs and began tracing the red tulip pattern on the tablecloth she had brought over from Hungary.

"Listen to me, dear heart. You know we just want what's best for you. That's why we come to America. So our children can have better lives than us. So we need to talk about your future."

She set a bowl of thick pinkish soup in front of me. It smelled full of paprika.

"Start eating," she said. "I'll talk. You eat and listen."

I bent over the table and stirred my spoon around and around in the thick soup. Usually I love it, but now my throat closed up.

"First, I want to know about the test, Lara."

I stared at the soup. "What test?"

"Don't act dumb, Lara. The test the people give you last night. The people who pay for your dancing lessons."

"You mean the audition."

"My saints! Test. Audition. Did you pass?"

"Did you?" That was Apa in the doorway asking Mom's question all over again. My stomach clenched.

"Stop chewing your hair and answer us, Lara," Mom said.

"Well, no —"

"Then, that's that!" she said. "The last straw!"

I heard Apa rasp something in the doorway and sigh. "I should have known," he muttered, shaking his head sadly. "Not enough talent. Like me. Like Steve."

I turned frantically. "But, Apa, that's not true. I am talented." But he was gone.

"Now for sure, no more dancing lessons," Mom said.

I pressed my hand against my medal.

"But, Mom, Mrs. Martin thinks I'm talented." My words came out as quavery as Mr. Swensen's grace notes on the piano. "Mr. Markoff thinks I'm good, too. At least I think he does. Besides, the audition was for a different scholarship. One back in New York. It doesn't have anything to do with the one out here. Really, Mom, they'll keep on paying."

"My saints, you must think them people in New York are dumb. They're not going to keep on paying if you can't pass their test, or audition, or whatever you call it."

I slumped down. Was she right? I hadn't connected the two scholarships. I mean, since Summer and I didn't even make the finals, would the New York school stop paying for our lessons out here? I hugged my arms across my chest and let my hair swing forward to cover my face. Outside, Apa's van started wheezing. He was going to work after all.

"Lara, I said, don't you think it stands to reason that they won't pay if you don't have no talent?" Mom asked. "Answer me that!"

I could only shake my head. Tears came streaming.

"Well, I know they won't," Mom said. "And your father and me don't have no money except Steve's. And we sure aren't throwing that away on ballet lessons. Besides, it's not just the money, it's the time. Starting today, you're not wasting no more time dancing. You're staying home and doing your school work just like the rest of the nice young girls at St. Catherine's."

Chapter 8

Who cares about trig or the Spanish subjunctive when your whole life has gone down the tubes? No ballet classes since Monday. Four whole days without a glimpse of Peter's beautiful green eyes or his quick, uncertain smile that turns my stomach inside out.

Every day after school I would push away whatever I was supposed to be studying. Sometimes, using my dresser as a barre, I would try a few *pliés*, but my body was stiff and achy, and my foot still hurt a little where I bumped it. Usually, I just threw myself on my bed, clutched the rag doll Mom had made for me when I was little, and stared at the ceiling.

Did Steve feel like this when he was sent overseas? All his hopes, all his dreams wiped out. I had never really thought about him as a person before. What was he like?

Friday afternoon I wandered over to his cabinet. It's here in the room that used to be his and is now mine. Behind locked glass doors lie his baseball cards, Little League pictures and trophies, a thin bundle of letters, and a few souvenirs a buddy brought home from Vietnam after Steve died.

Suddenly Mom walked into my room. She never knocks.

"My saints, daydreaming again. And look at the mess this room is in. Done all your school work yet?"

"What? Oh, not all of it, Mom. It's Friday. I have all weekend."

"Well, I don't want the sisters sending home no more notes. So get to it. What was you staring at Steve's things for?"

"Just looking. I hardly remember Steve at all. I was only four when he got drafted. What was he like?"

"Like?" Her face crumpled. Her eyes squinted and shone with tears. Her mouth puckered like an apple you've forgotten in the refrigerator for three months. "Steve was good. Got good grades, too. Wish yours was half as good."

I stiffened. "Maybe I'm not good at school work but I'm good at ballet."

"Humph! That why you didn't get that scholarship you wanted so bad?"

"But I told you why."

"Don't talk to me in that whiny voice. Do your school work now. I got to go to the store before your dad gets home and wants his supper."

After she left, I went into my folks' room

and took the tiny brass cabinet key off her dresser. I had the right to know something about my own brother, didn't I?

The key bent in the lock but the cabinet doors swung open. I pulled out Steve's baseball cards. They were slick and oily from much shuffling and trading with kids at school and down the block.

I didn't recognize any of the players on the cards but he probably knew every face, just as I know all the important dancers. Even I knew a name I saw below one of the pictures, though. Joe DiMaggio. Maybe Steve dreamed of becoming another DiMaggio like I dream of becoming another Cynthia Gregory.

I brought out his two Little League Trophies. They're ugly, but Steve must have loved them. They're exactly alike, made of metal, each with its own block of wood to stand on. Both little players consist of two soldered-together parts. My fingers pressed the rough seams. *Scars.* I shuddered. One pedestal says, *Player with the Best Attendance, 1964.* The other says, *Player with the Most Heart, 1965.*

There's no award for *Best Pitcher* or *Best Fielder* or *Best All Around Player.* Nothing like that. I guess Steve didn't have much talent for baseball. Maybe that's why Mom thinks — and maybe Apa, too — I'm not talented at ballet. But I am. I know I am.

Sighing, I thrust my hand into the cabinet again. Here was one of Steve's Little League photographs. The whole team's in bulky uniforms. Steve's is miles too big. He's looking down shyly, but his chest is out and he's grinning. You can tell he's really proud.

Returning the photograph, I lifted out the thin pack of letters and removed the rubber band holding it. The top envelope was dated October 9, 1972, the day before he died. In large, angular handwriting, it was addressed to Mr. and Mrs. Frank Havas.

The envelope opened flat, the back forming a flimsy sheet for writing. It was half covered with the sharp ups and downs of Steve's letters.

Dear Mom and Dad, Not much going on here. Just waiting around for action in this stinking jungle. It rains and rains. Mud everywhere. Rifles rusting. I miss you. Wish I'd got good grades and made you proud. I promise to do better.
Your son, Steve.

Poor Steve! Imagine worrying about grades the day before he was killed. Tears came to my eyes. I was too sad to read more letters. Besides, Mom might come back any minute. I locked the cabinet and returned the key. Would she notice it was bent? I hid it under the frame of Steve's Army photo.

Then I looked at the picture. Unless you really studied it, he seemed almost the same kid he was in the Little League photo. Posed in front of an American flag, he was taller but still thin. The uniform hung on him. His neck rose, long and skinny, out of the jacket.

His eyes were different, though. They were wide open with the whites showing all around the gray iris. Maybe it was only the glare of the photographer's light, but he looked terrified.

Next to Steve's photograph was an old newspaper picture of John F. Kennedy. It had turned brown inside the black dime store frame that matched the one holding my brother's picture. Under the President's were words from *Ecclesiastes* that were read at Kennedy's funeral mass. And at Steve's.

To everything there is a season / And a time to every purpose under the heaven /, A time to be born, and a time to die.

The lines stopped there. Mom must have cut off the rest of the quotation to make the clipping fit the frame. Somewhere in the middle, though, there was a line I had heard Father López recite to Mom several years after Steve died.

"Remember, Mrs. Havas, there's 'a time to mourn, and a time to dance.' "

I sighed. A time to dance! I wished Father López were here now to tell Mom that again and mean it in more ways than one. Maybe Summer would, if I could get hold of her.

I ran to the kitchen and picked up the

phone. It was still dead. Today after Spanish class I had tried to call her from the pay phone outside the office. There was no answer. I felt so cut off.

But now somebody was stabbing our doorbell. When I got to the front door, there stood Summer.

She was smiling, her face glowing from the inside like a jack-o-lantern after Apa scrapes out the pulp and flesh of the pumpkin so that the candle flame shines through the rind.

"Girl, am I ever glad to see you. You been sick? Sure doesn't look it. I've got a zillion things to tell you. Remember Stephanie's shoes? The expensive suede pumps? Well, they disappeared during the storm. Mad? You better believe it! She blames Daniel and Daniel blames the San José State students. They're back from vacation now. Hot dog! Stephanie's car's okay. Or going to be. It's in the garage getting fixed."

Summer took a quick breath, then rushed on. "We still can't use the room the tree smashed through but the big studio's okay now. They cleared out the mud and junk so we're taking class there. If you aren't sick, why haven't you been coming?"

It was so great to see and hear Summer that for a minute I forgot all my problems. Then I remembered.

"I — I can't go to ballet anymore." I didn't add, *and I can't see Peter*, but I thought it.

"Why not, for gosh sake?"

"No scholarship."

"What do you mean, no scholarship?"

I hunted in my jeans' pockets for a Kleenex, blew my nose, and explained everything.

"That's just crazy!" Summer said when I got it all out. "Our scholarships are good till June. They're completely separate from that stupid audition. So get your tote bag and let's get going. Stephanie's waiting in the truck."

"But my folks think I'm wasting my time taking ballet. Even Apa. They say I haven't got any talent."

"Course, you have talent. A scholarship, too. Come on."

I backed up against Old Magyar. "I can't, Summer."

"Lord, I'll talk to them then."

"They aren't home."

"Your dad is. He drove up just before we did. He's out there yakking to Stephanie. Go get your things while I persuade him."

Summer danced out the door. I heard her clippity-clipping down the front steps. I grabbed my things and followed.

Stephanie Martin peered out of the truck and Summer stood beside it talking to Apa. I don't know who was gesturing most.

"Get a move on, Lara!" Summer yelled. "We're going to be late."

I looked quickly at Apa. His eyes shone black above his mustache.

"Summer's right. You are keeping Mrs. Martin waiting, little one. They say you still have a scholarship and that it's money wasted if you don't take the lessons."

"But what about Mom?" I asked Apa.

Apa shrugged. "She doesn't like wasting money any more than I do. So you will take lessons until your scholarship is used up."

Chapter 9

Rush hour traffic jammed the freeway. Mrs. Martin took side streets to Markoff's. When we arrived, I didn't see Peter. Sometimes he's late or doesn't come because three days a week he works out in the gym.

Mr. Swensen came into the foyer with a stack of music under one arm. He couldn't return our waves and smiles because he was coughing.

"He's had that cold all week," Summer said. "Ever since the storm."

We went down the hall to the dressing room. Still no Peter, but it was really good to be back even if the whole place did stink of mold and damp wood. Meredith followed us into the girls' dressing room.

"You been sick or something, Lara? We really missed you. Me and Peter."

I turned my back. "I didn't know he was here today," I said, trying to sound casual.

"Oh, sure. We've been warming up in the little studio, if you know what I mean."

I cringed.

"Here we go again," said another girl in our class, brushing her hair in front of the mirror. "Even before we have time to say welcome back to Lara."

"Yeah, knock it off, Meredith," Summer said. "We're a little bored with hearing about your sexual exploits."

"Well, if you're going to be snotty, Summer, I won't say what I came in especially to tell you. Something that would really interest you."

Summer bent double to adjust the ribbons of her *pointe* shoes. "Oh, yeah?" she said.

"Yes," Meredith said, and began spilling the latest studio gossip.

"A new student just came in to take class. You should see him, Summer. His name is Jason Duval. He's twenty. A modern dancer who's studied at San Francisco Ballet School, too. He's down here to take modern at San José State. Says he's danced in a bunch of musicals. He's a little taller than Lara. Good-looking. Anyway, he's black and just moved in upstairs."

Silence. Finally someone said, "Sounds like you should start a dating service or something, Meredith."

Meredith sniffed. "I just thought Summer might be interested since she's always panting after the roomers upstairs."

Summer shot her a look as cold as one of Mrs. Martin's. "Now that sounds more like the old Meredith we all know and love. You must really have been pumping the poor dude. What do you expect me to do, fling myself into his arms?"

"Well, that's the last favor I do you, Summer Jones," Meredith said, and pranced out.

Summer kicked her jeans and T-shirt under the bench. "Wish that was her butt I was kicking! Be back in a sec, Lara."

She was and began pawing through her tote bag. First, she came up with a pink satin ribbon and tied it around her throat. Next she found her lipstick and dabbed some on. Finally, she pulled out a bottle of cologne and really doused herself with it.

"Did you see him, Summer?" somebody asked.

"Obviously, " I said, giggling. "But don't you think you're sort of overdoing the cologne, Summer?"

"No way. For once, I owe creepy Meredith one. He ain't bad. Ain't bad atall!"

Then she was off again and down the hall.

"Wait for me," I called.

But she kept going until she reached the studio door. There she stopped. I mean, suddenly. So suddenly that I crashed into her.

"Oops, sorry," she said.

"How come you're stopping?"

She rolled her eyes. "To shift gears. What else?"

I laughed. "Where is he? I can't see him."

"Against the wall in front of Meredith and Peter."

"Oh." I didn't want Peter to think I was staring at him so I stayed in the doorway and peeked around Summer. My glance didn't get as far as Jason, though. It stopped at Peter's shoulders swelling under his thin T-shirt and at his firm buttocks under skin-tight nylon trunks. His white legs tensed in a warm-up stretch. I leaned against the door frame, trembling.

Finally, I guess Summer figured she had waited long enough. She arched her back and floated across the floor. The ends of the pink ribbon fluttered behind her. The sweetness of her cologne wafted through the room.

But did she go stand next to the new student? No way! She took her regular place beside me in front of one of the bay windows. The entire length of the studio stretched between them. She did *pliés*, then *frappés*, and apparently didn't glance at him even in the mirror. I did, though. Right in front of Peter's tall, sturdy reflection, stood Jason's. Medium height. Awesome thighs and shoulders. Smooth, curvy muscles. Sucked-in waist. Relaxed mouth. Nose sharp as a knife. Shiny black skin. Golly, they were opposites, Peter and Jason! Both heart-stopping!

"Did you see him?" Summer whispered. "Girl, he's a real hunk of man!"

Even then she didn't look at him, though. But he was staring at her. I sighed, wishing

Peter would stare at me like that.

All during class Summer showed absolutely no interest in this Jason Duval but she danced better than I had ever seen her. She soared, spun, flickered her feet. Not me, though. After no ballet for almost a week, I stumbled, gasped, and nearly had to stop before class was over. When it did end, I headed straight for the dressing room.

Summer caught hold of my arm. "This way, Lara, through the foyer."

"How come? I don't want to run into Peter and Meredith."

"They went into the hall," she said, and I knew where they were heading: the little back studio. "Come on," Summer said. "Quit stalling."

Sighing, I tagged after Summer into the dim foyer. When I caught up, she was chattering to Meredith's housekeeper. As far as I knew, this was the first time Summer had even spoken to the woman.

"Meredith will be right out, Mrs. Mueller, ma'am. Wasn't that storm last Sunday something else?"

Mrs. Mueller scowled. "Tell her to hurry."

"Certainly, ma'am," Summer said. "I'll tell her right away, ma'am."

Her attention seemed totally on this woman, none left over for Jason Duval. He had come into the foyer, too, and stationed himself near the drinking fountain.

"And have a really good evening, Mrs. Mueller, hear?"

Summer turned away. Her eyes gleamed at me.

"Wait up, Lara. I've got to have me a drink of water before I die of thirst."

She didn't look at Jason standing by the fountain. She just quick bent over the porcelain basin and reached for the handle to turn on the water.

"Please allow me," he said with such a low bow that his forehead brushed his knees. I mean, was he ever exaggerating! His voice was deep and mellow and so full of laughter that I expected him to burst into loud guffaws. I guess he was playing the same game as Summer.

She looked startled, wide-eyed. She fanned her lashes. "Why, thank you, sir." She waited for him to turn on the fountain.

Then, just as she was dipping her mouth into the clear arc of water, Stephanie Martin burst through one of the double front doors. A blast of winter air blew in with her.

"Summer Jones, how many times have I told you not to drink water when you are over-heated?"

Probably Mrs. Martin was the last person in the world Summer wanted to see. She faced her smiling, though.

"Sorry, Stephanie. I got really thirsty. Mr. Markoff's class was super hard tonight."

"Well, wet your mouth, if you must, but don't swallow any water."

Then Mrs. Martin spotted Jason. For a second she gaped as if she had seen him someplace before. A frown creased her smooth forehead. Her cheeks got hollower.

"And may I ask who you are?" Her question was ice cold. Which didn't seem to bother him in the least. He grinned at her. "That's okay, lady. Ask away. I'm Jason Duval. Down from San Francisco."

"I see," was all she said, but the look she gave him would have shriveled me. Jason held out a broad black hand for her to shake.

"You must be Summer's mother," he said.

Stephanie Martin ignored his hand. "I am not Summer's mother. I am her mentor. And Lara's." She turned her back on Jason and snapped at us, "Get dressed, both of you. Be ready to leave in ten minutes. I want to be home at a reasonable hour tonight. Daniel deserves dinner on time for once."

She whirled away and vanished into Mr. Markoff's office under the stairs. We stared after her, silently at first. Then Summer burst into giggles. So did I, a little nervously to begin with. We bent double and choked with laughter. Jason smiled and watched us. He pocketed the hand he had put out for Stephanie to shake.

"Oh, what a crack-up!" Summer said.

"Did I say something wrong?" His eyes glittered almost as much as Summer's.

"As if you didn't know. Stephanie's a bit young to be my mother, unless, of course," she added, her eyes gleaming at me, "unless she and Blackbird had had a kid."

Jason's eyebrows lifted. "Shall we discuss all this over Cokes?" he asked.

She shook her head. "Thanks an awful lot, Jason. But we can't with Stephanie waiting. In a really rotten mood, too, thanks to you. Is she my mother? Lord, she'll never ever forgive you. But yes, some other time we'd love to have Cokes with you. Is she my mother? Oh, Lord!"

Still laughing, we went into the hall. Then, right away I stopped laughing and stood still. I couldn't believe what I was seeing. Halfway between the two dressing rooms Meredith clung to Peter. While I watched, she stretched her arms around his neck and kissed him full and long on the mouth. Then she laughed and bounced into the girls' dressing room.

I stared at Peter. He glanced at me, then away again. His face turned red. His palms rubbed up and down his white thighs as if hunting for pockets to sink his hands into. Finally, he dived into the men's dressing room. I crept into the girls'. Changing as fast as I could, I pretended not to hear Meredith and Rosemary laughing hysterically in the far corner.

"Listen, Lara," Summer said after we were dressed and heading for Stephanie Martin's truck, "if you want your muscle man back, quit moping and do something about it."

On the ride home Mrs. Martin stared

straight ahead. No singing this trip! A few blocks from my house she said, "Summer, I'm curious to know what exactly was going on at the ballet school tonight."

"Can't I get a drink of water? That's all I was doing. Ask Lara."

I nodded so hard that my hair slipped out of its topknot and came tumbling in a brown shower around my shoulders.

Mrs. Martin glared straight ahead. Her hands squeezed the steering wheel. "He's too old for you, Summer."

"Lord, Stephanie, all he did was turn on the drinking fountain for me! We aren't eloping or anything."

Summer giggled. I didn't dare to with Mrs. Martin looking so uptight. She went on as if she hadn't heard Summer.

"You're fifteen. He's twenty-one."

"He's twenty," Summer said.

"I happened to see his school registration card, sweetheart. It happened to be on Mr. Markoff's desk. He happens to be twenty-one."

"Okay. Okay. Not that I like him or anything, but what're a few years difference? Daniel's ten whole years older than you."

Stephanie gave a short laugh. "I was twenty-three when we met at George Washington University. Age differences don't matter so much then."

Summer turned her face slowly toward Mrs. Martin.

"Now I get it. Blackbird! You were my age when you ran off with Blackbird. How old was he? Twenty-one?"

I glanced sideways at Mrs. Martin, then sank back against the seat. She looked as if she were about to explode. Cheeks and mouth sucked in. Eyes glinting with sparks.

"I don't know what Blackbird, as you call him, has to do with it. All I know is that Jason is too old for you. And too flashy! You need to concentrate on ballet!"

Chapter 10

When Mrs. Martin dropped me off at my house, there stood Mom under our porch light. Short and stubby, she reminded me of a pawn in Apa's chess set. Her arms clutched her chest. Without saying a word, she watched my feet mounting the steps.

"Uh, hi, Mom. I hope you weren't worried. Apa said it was okay for me to go to ballet."

"Humph! Spose he said it was okay to get into Steve's cabinet, too."

She held out the twisted key. I hunched my shoulders.

"Well, did he?"

I shook my head.

"And now the key's all crooked, bent out of shape."

"Who's bent out of shape?" Apa asked in the doorway. "You, Liska?"

She waggled the key in his face. "This here's what's out of shape, Frank. The key to Steve's cabinet. Lara bent it."

Apa reached for it. "Give it to me. I'll fix it."

Mom snatched the key away and snorted. "You? Like you fixed the squeaky board in the porch?"

"I said, give it here. Making such a fuss over a little key!"

Mom handed it over, then lowered her voice. "It isn't just the key," she said, her mouth trembling. "It's her getting into Steve's things, then going off to dancing when all the time she should of been doing her school work."

Apa pushed the key into his pocket and put his arm around her. "There, there, Liska, don't cry. She didn't mean to upset you. Let her alone."

Wiping her eyes on her apron, Mom crossed the porch.

"All I want is for her to get good grades, Frank."

Apa closed the front door behind us. "She gets good grades, Liska."

"That's all you know."

I inched toward my room.

"Aren't your grades going to be good on your report card next week, little one?" Apa asked.

I pressed my back against the wall. "Uh, they're A's and B's, I think."

"B's?" Mom said. "B's aren't good enough. If you want to get into a good college, the sisters say you shouldn't be getting nothing but A's. Like Steve."

I glanced at her. Like Steve? But after reading his letter, I knew his grades weren't nearly as good as she was always claiming.

Apa lowered himself into Old Magyar.

"B's are fine," he said. "B's will get Lara into a good college. But get less than a B, Lara, then no more dancing, scholarship or no."

By some miracle, I received B's — and even one A — on my report card at the end of January, so Mom let me alone for a few weeks. Then, early in February, I got a C on a test on the Spanish subjunctive. I hid the paper, but Mom found it when she went snooping through my binder.

At supper she waved my test paper in Apa's face.

"Now I suppose you're going to say a C is a B."

He frowned at the paper, then at me. "What did we agree, Lara? All A's and B's, wasn't it?"

"But, Apa! This is only a little Friday quiz."

"Little quiz or big, you must receive at least B's if you are to continue ballet. You have until next week to better that grade in Spanish."

Mom grunted and stomped over to the stove. "Till next week! Till next week! You're too easy on her, Frank."

All next week I studied Spanish really hard. It paid off. I made a B-plus on the quiz next Friday.

I was working hard at ballet, too. More than ever I knew I had to become a dancer. I couldn't be at the studio the whole afternoon the way Summer and Meredith were, but I talked the nuns into letting me practice ballet instead of taking PE. And to reach Markoff's in time for Mrs. Martin's four o'clock class, I rushed to the bus stop the minute trig was over, and didn't even take time to change out of my scratchy uniform into jeans. Afterward, Summer and I, and Meredith, too, worked an hour before advanced class.

Peter, however, never practiced or took extra classes, not even on Saturdays when Mrs. Martin usually stayed around to coach us. One Saturday in the middle of February she had to leave right after she finished teaching.

"Daniel's getting some kind of engineering award this noon and wants me to attend the luncheon," she told us while we were waiting to take the advanced class. "Mr. Markoff says you may stay and practice if you lock up afterwards."

Summer and I watched Mrs. Martin leave. She wore a perfectly-cut black wool suit and diamonds in her ears.

"Come on," Summer said as soon as Mrs. Martin was gone. "While she can't object, let's go take class beside my man."

I tilted my head. *"Your man?* Good grief! I never even thought of calling Peter that and you've only known Jason two weeks."

"We're fast operators, me and Jason. Off alone in the back studio, we don't exactly work on *pirouettes*. More like *pas de deux*." She giggled. "Your eyes're big as saucers. Don't look so surprised."

I wasn't surprised. I was sad, wistful. I chewed a lock of hair. Peter and I never got beyond holding hands.

All during class Summer and I worked beside Jason. I was aware, though, of Peter across the room, lowering his magnificent legs in *pliés*, spreading them in *grands jetés*, or crossing one over the other while he sagged against the barre between combinations.

After class all the kids left except Summer and me. Usually Meredith remained, too, but this afternoon, framed in the doorway, she fluttered her fingers at us. "Tah-tah! Sorry to leave you nerds. But I've got a heavy date with Peter."

"Creep!" I muttered, but my stomach clenched.

I was still scowling after Meredith when Mr. Markoff came to the door. "Everyone else has gone now, girls. So I'll lock the inner doors. Don't let anyone in. Not even the San José State students."

"Lord, this place is like living behind the iron curtain," Summer said. "Upstairs is out-of-bounds for us. The ballet school is out-of-bounds for them."

Mr. Markoff shrugged. "Sorry. Work hard now."

"Sure thing," Summer said. But as soon

as we heard Mr. Markoff's car roar out the driveway she said, "Let's go."

"Where? Aren't we going to practice?"

"Not now. We've got a date with Jason."

"We?"

"Yes, we. We're supposed to meet him at the ice cream parlor."

I hung back. "Listen, Summer, I'm not tagging along on your date."

"It's not *my* date. It's *our* date. Like when we both used to go for ice cream with Peter."

"That was different. Then we were all friends. All three of us."

"Oh, give me a break, girl. It was you he liked."

"Do you really think he did Summer?" I sighed. "Anyway, I'm not coming. I wouldn't feel right. Jason's not an old friend like Peter."

Summer bit her thumbnail and looked away. She untied and kicked off one of her *pointe* shoes. "That's partly why I want you along, Lara. I'd feel lots more comfortable."

"What do you mean, more comfortable?" But she wouldn't meet my eyes. Summer, of all people! She usually stares practically into my soul.

"Well, something happened." She still wouldn't look at me. Just kept winding the ribbons around the soft, folded-in heel of one of her *pointe* shoes. I was getting worried.

"For gosh sakes, what happened?"

But before she could answer, down the hall came a rumbling voice, bellowing "Ain't Misbehavin'." Jason! Now, how did he get back inside the ballet school?

He strode into the classroom still in tights and T-shirt, looking very masculine. Somehow, in the empty studio, he seemed even more masculine than usual. I mean, wow!

"Take pity on a poor stowaway," he boomed. His arms made sweeping, operatic gestures. His voice filled the room.

"Jason! We're supposed to meet you at the ice cream parlor," Summer said. She was laughing but her voice shook a little.

"I know, baby."

Baby! First she calls him *my man.* Now he calls her *baby!* I couldn't believe it!

"Who wants to wait around all alone upstairs, baby? So I stowed away in the can. Tucked up my feet when the big man checked to be sure everyone was out of the dressing room. Thought we might do a little close dancin' now that Dragon Lady's split."

His laughter rolled out. He swooped down and swept Summer up into his arms. Backing against the barre, I began collecting my towel, sweater, soft ballet shoes, legwarmers, all my belongings.

Summer squealed and kicked her feet. "Jason, put me down."

He didn't. She kicked a little harder but not very hard. Soon she just cuddled against him and asked softly, "Don't you think you should put me down, Jason honey?"

"Uh, guess I'll go get dressed," I said, flying to the door.

"Hey! Wait up," Summer shouted. She struggled out of Jason's arms. "Let's get dressed and all go to the ice cream parlor together, okay?"

In the dressing room, I turned to her. "All right, Summer, what's going on?"

"I would have told you before, Lara, but it only happened last night."

I squealed. "What did?"

"Well, after you left to catch your bus, Jason pushed a note into my hand."

"He what?" We both collapsed on the bench, giggling, heads together.

"That's right, girl!"

"So what did the note say?"

"Said to meet him at the top of the stairs soon as I could."

More giggles. "Good grief. Did you?"

She nodded. Just the thought of meeting Peter like that and being held in his strong warm arms turned my insides to jelly. "Then what happened?" I asked.

"We went into his room and shut the door."

I let out another shriek. Summer covered my mouth. "Sh-sh-sh! He'll hear you."

She stopped giggling and poked out her lip. The dressing room was so quiet I could hear her breathing. I shook the bobby pins out of my hair. In the year and a half that Peter and I were friends, he never asked me to meet him alone.

"So, uh, did anything happen up in Jason's room?" I asked.

"Well, we talked a while, joked around like always, then he started telling me how crazy he was about me. Loved me, he said. Had since the first night he came to class."

She slid a little ways down the bench and unwound her toe shoe ribbons. I stared at her. I mean, what was she going to say next?

"I don't know if I should tell you this, Lara."

My face got hot and I thought about what Mom and the sisters say about bodily sins. "Oh, well, if you don't want to, Summer. I mean, I'd understand. Honestly."

"Lord, girl, it's nothing like that. We didn't do anything. Not really. But what's so scary is that I wanted to go right ahead and have sex with Jason. No precautions. No nothing. I was almost glad to hear Stephanie downstairs calling me. So you just have to come along with us now, Lara. Cause I'm scared that if I get left alone with him I might do something stupid."

"In the ice cream parlor?"

Summer giggled. "No, silly. But I want us to stay in the ice cream parlor. Not go back up to his room. I want it like it used to be with you and me and Peter. All three of us having fun together."

I nodded sadly. "Me, too." But was that really all I wanted? "Did Mrs. Martin catch you?" I asked.

"Nope. I sneaked back downstairs while

she was searching the dressing rooms. Later, though, when she was giving me the third degree, I just told her I'd been in the john the whole time. 'Got my period,' I said."

Both of us cracked up, but stopped laughing when someone began pounding on the dressing room door.

"Be out in two minutes, ladies, or I'm coming in."

Of course, it was Jason.

Chapter 11

Summer had to run to keep up with Jason on the way to the ice cream parlor. Even I had to really stretch my legs. He strode between us, glittering with energy. His feet seemed made of soft rubber. They bounced off the sidewalk. I nearly expected him to sail into a *grand jeté*, and leap over the sun that was just now shining through the thin clouds.

At the intersection he said, "Come fly with me, ladies." And holding hands, laughing, the three of us sprinted across the street.

"You're crazy, Jason!" Summer said. Her eyes were golden. Her face shone from inside. He caught her to him in a quick hug.

"And you're something else!" he said. His chest rumbled. He hummed "Ain't Misbehavin'" again.

It was obvious he liked Summer a lot. And she liked him. It was also obvious that I was in the way.

I hurried ahead of them and into the ice cream parlor. They came right behind.

"Sit down, sit down," Jason called. He waved an arm toward the scatter of round pink tables. Acted as if he owned all of them. Only one was empty. I sat down, twisted my legs back under my chair, and wound my arms across my chest. If I could only disappear!

At the counter Summer bobbed beside Jason. She's little and cute and seemed pulled to him like metal to a magnet. She stood with her left arm pressed against his right. They poked each other, looped arms around each other's waists, pointed at the cartons of ice cream behind the glass counter. Giggled. Laughed.

I had to look away. Was I jealous? Or only longing for Peter?

"You want a hot fudge sundae, Lara?" Summer called. "That's what we're having."

We! The *we* meant Summer and Jason. Not Summer and me. Not even Summer, Jason, and me. Tears stung my eyes. *We* used to mean Summer, Peter, and me.

I nodded yes to her question. If I tried to say anything I'd start crying.

I put on a big brave smile when they paraded toward the table carrying the sundaes. Summer set one in front of me. "Dah-DAH!" The sundae was enormous. A mountain of shiny brown chocolate. Whipped cream on top of that. Last, a cherry.

Jason set down the two sundaes he was carrying, then pulled two chairs close together, so close that when he and Summer sat down their shoulders touched. An empty chair on each side separated me from them still further. As if I weren't lonely enough already!

"Well, here go our diets!" I said brightly. Too brightly. I stirred my sundae until it was tan soup. Yuk! It looked gross.

Across from me Summer and Jason talked nonsense. They sang, laughed, fed each other. I might as well have been a stranger, sitting with them because there was no vacant table.

Suddenly, Summer stopped laughing. Her eyes widened. "Well, will you look at who just come in!"

"*Came* in," Jason corrected. He nudged her with his elbow and laughed hugely. "I'm standing in for Dragon Lady this afternoon, so y'all better mind your grammar, hear?"

But Summer didn't giggle or nudge him back. She frowned and looked from me to the door. I looked, too. My face burned. I hunched down and twisted my legs tighter around the chair legs. For into the ice cream parlor came Meredith and Peter.

Fortunately, they didn't see us in the crowd. At least not yet.

Meredith minced ahead a few steps, then, laughing and chattering, waited for Peter to catch up. He strode in, his strong legs encased in tight jeans. My stomach tightened.

"Uh, guess I'll be going," I said. Maybe I could clear out before Peter and Meredith saw me.

"You stay put, Lara Havas," Summer said. "If you want Peter, it's about time you did something."

"Like what?"

"We're all friends, more or less, aren't we?" Summer asked. "So invite them to join us."

I hunched down in my chair. "I'd die."

Jason grinned at me. "Nothing to it, Lara baby." He leaped up. One arm swept great circles in the air. "Over here, Peter and Meredith," he boomed.

They looked at us. I sank lower on my spine. Meredith was talking right into Peter's face and waving her hands. Obviously, she was objecting to something and you didn't have to be a straight-A student like Summer to know what. Meredith was refusing to sit with us. Well, what did I expect?

Summer giggled. "Ten to one, Meredith wins out. And you, girl, stop acting like a shrinking violet. Pull yourself together!" Suddenly she stiffened. "I don't believe it! They're coming over. So play it cool, Lara."

"Little Miss Fix-it," Jason said, laughing.

I hardly breathed.

Meredith waggled toward our table, swinging her narrow hips and wavy blonde hair. Peter followed, wearing an embarrassed grin and a red face. He frowned at the ice cream cone and soda that he clutched, one in each hand. Was he the one, then, who hadn't wanted to sit with us? Of course, there weren't many empty tables to choose from this afternoon.

"Uh, how's it going?" he asked, not looking at us. On the table between Summer and me, he set down the soda. It was mint-flavored with a tiny green parasol riding on top. He stalked behind me and sat in the empty chair between Jason and me. He licked his cone.

I stayed very still and played it very cool. Peter's arms, unlike his legs which never get any sun, were a golden tan below the sleeves of his T-shirt. The closest one didn't quite touch me but I could feel its warmth. I took a quick breath and tried to relax.

Meredith stood behind me, curling her short pink fingers around the cane back of my chair. "I'd really like to be by Peter, you know, Lara, since we're on a date," she said sweetly. "You don't mind changing places with me, do you?"

"Don't you dare move, Lara Havas!" Summer said under her breath.

She didn't have to tell me that, for gosh sakes. I wasn't about to move.

Meredith's face went scarlet. Which must have been about the shade mine was. She fidgeted with the tiny green parasol from her soda and finally forced it too far. Its toothpick ribs snapped.

"I'm going to find us another table, Peter, like I wanted to in the first place."

So it was Meredith, after all, who hadn't wanted to sit with us. I tried not to look too happy.

"Uh, there aren't any vacant tables," Peter said, frowning and licking his ice cream. The hand not holding the cone went into his pocket.

"There are so!" Meredith said. "The bus boy's clearing off a table by the window right now."

"Well, I think I'll just stay here," he said slowly. He licked his cone where it was beginning to melt.

My heart was thudding in my ears. I sipped a spoonful of soupy ice cream. It didn't taste as gross as it looked!

"Well, I'm moving," Meredith said.

She picked up her soda but left the crumpled green parasol on our table. "Coming, Peter?" Her voice, sharp at first, began to wheedle. "It's sunny by the window, Peter. Besides, they probably want to be alone just as much as we do. At least, Summer and Jason do."

Peter tightened his free hand into a fist. He was looking down so I wasn't able to see his eyes.

"I'm staying here, if nobody minds," he said, and flashed his eyes at me. They were so green, so clear that I forgot to breathe.

"Sure, that's great, Peter," I murmured.

"In that case, Peter Hanson," Meredith snapped, "you can stay here all afternoon for all I care. You can have this old soda, too."

She set down her glass and gave it a shove. It wobbled, tottered, and finally toppled. It sloshed a bright green river across the pink marble table top. We all four leaped up and began mopping at the flood with our paper napkins. The bus boy rushed to our rescue with a towel. When the table was clean again and I had time to look around, Meredith was gone.

I was half afraid that Peter would trudge after her, but he didn't. He stayed and, while his tongue came out to lap his ice cream cone, the golden fuzz on the big forearm closest to me tickled my skin. Thrills sped through me.

"Well, Jason and I have got to be going," Summer said.

"Going?" I asked.

"Yes. To buy new *pointe* shoes. You know how hopeless my old ones are. Jason's coming along to help."

Jason's laugh rumbled. "Yeah, I'm the world's greatest expert on *pointe* shoes."

They stood up to leave. I swallowed. I sure hoped Peter wouldn't think I'd planned this whole thing just to get him alone.

I looked at his broad red face, the frown between his eyes, the wide shoulders straining against the thin cotton of his T-shirt. Even in winter he's never cold. And I'm always freezing.

Summer beamed at us. "See y'all later. Bet you've got lots to talk about."

Maybe we had but after Summer and Jason left, we stared at the table. Peter slid his hands into the pockets of his jeans, then out, then in again. He cleared his throat and muttered, "Hey, Lara, she's right. We do have things to talk about. Like, well, why you've been avoiding me, running away."

"Running away?" I nearly choked on the question. My eyes opened wide. "Me?"

He nodded slowly. "Yes, you."

I stared at him. My lips trembled. "But I haven't, Peter. Really."

Silence. I finally asked, "What makes you say I run away?"

"Well, that's how it seems to me. Like just now. And it's been the same way ever since I went to that silly dance with Meredith."

Tears rose to my eyes and words I didn't mean to say burst out. "So if the dance was so silly, why did you go?"

He frowned. "Don't be like that. You sound like her."

"Like who?"

"Meredith. Bossy. I didn't want to go to the dance, Lara. What happened is I sort of got forced into it. She didn't really ask me. She asked my mom. I was at the gym when she phoned. So when I got home Mom said I'd been invited to this so-called harvest dance and why didn't I go. She said this fancy girls' school of Meredith's was giving it and it might help me become more relaxed in what Mom calls social situations. You know how she talks, being a psychologist and all."

"So you went," I said, sucking on an end of my hair.

"Yes, but it was a drag. I had to rent a tux and couldn't get one that fit because my shoulders had got so big. That's one of the reasons I quit lifting weights."

"You quit?" I asked, amazed. "Why?"

He shrugged. "It was a drag going to the gym all the time. Working my rear off. Then my dad goes and asks what I'm trying to do, become Mr. Universe or something? If I put in the same amount of time on homework, he says, I might have a chance of getting into engineering school."

I sighed. "I'm really sorry, Peter. Parents can sure be pains!" I leaned closer to him, but he kept licking his ice cream.

"Anyway, that monkey suit I rented was so tight I could hardly breathe. The ballroom at the hotel was really stuffy, too. Smelled like a funeral parlor. You know, all the perfume and corsages."

"Corsages?" The word stuck in my throat. Roses? An orchid maybe? I wet my lips. "I suppose you had to give Meredith a corsage."

"Well, yes. But my mom took care of the whole thing. Ordered it from the florist, picked it up, did everything but pin it on Meredith's shoulder."

With a long, shaky forefinger I traced the squiggly lines in the fake marble table top.

"What was it?" I asked.

"What was what?"

"The corsage."

"Some kind of flower. I don't know."

"Was it an orchid?"

"I guess so. What does it matter? It was all my mom's doing."

I nodded but a tear slid down one cheek. A gauzy orchid, fragile as a butterfly, perched on Meredith's shoulder. Nobody had ever given me any kind of flower, let alone an orchid.

He frowned. "Awh, Lara, did I say something wrong? How come you're crying?" He craned around to see, I guess, if people were noticing my tears. "Like I said, I hated the whole thing."

Tears were pouring down my face now. My voice wobbled and I sort of hiccupped. "So — so how come you've been going with her ever since?"

His face flamed, but he didn't look at me. He licked ice cream dribbling down the side of his cone.

"Well, because you didn't seem to like me anymore, you know, Lara."

I shook my head back and forth. My hair flopped forward over my cheeks. "What was I supposed to do? You're always hanging out with her. I couldn't just barge in. Now you're even going to New York with her."

"Not *with* her. We're just both going. And, hey, Lara," he said, turning to me. A sudden smile lit his face and turned his eyes a clear chartreuse. "Maybe I won't go to New York. I'm not really big on it, especially if you and I get to be friends again."

I smiled. "I'd really like that, Peter."

"Hey, all right! Then it's settled!"

He grabbed me around the waist and hugged me against his huge, warm chest. I wanted to stay there forever.

Chapter 12

Maybe it sounds dumb, but ever since the afternoon Peter and I made up, everything in my life seems to have a special shimmer. It's like the bright web of angel hair Mom stretches over our Christmas tree each year.

This shimmer makes even ordinary things in my life seem wonderful. Like waking up in the morning. Now the minute I open my eyes I think, *Today I get to see Peter! Maybe today's the day he'll kiss me.* Because, while he hugs me a lot, he hasn't kissed me yet.

"Why not, do you think?" I asked Summer once.

"Girl, if you want Peter to kiss you, let him know it. Better yet, you kiss him. That's what Meredith did, among other things. She's been around."

Summer sighed and turned away. "But then Meredith doesn't have to live with Stephanie Martin!"

Summer has real problems of her own these days. For instance, last Saturday when

I arrived in the dressing room she didn't even say hi.

"What's wrong, Summer?"

She stuck out her lower lip. "What isn't? This time Stephanie caught me sneaking up to Jason's room."

"Good grief!"

"You can say that again. I'm grounded. Can't even take phone calls. Not to mention not being allowed within miles of Jason!"

Mrs. Martin came to the dressing room door. "Summer, I want you in the classroom. Now. You may put on your *pointe* shoes out there. And next time wear a regulation leotard, not that custom job you've cut the back out of."

Mr. Markoff lets us alter our leotards if we want to. I even persuaded Mom to sew crisscross straps down the back of mine. Summer cut hers clear down to the waist but Meredith's is so low it nearly shows her buns.

Summer glared at Mrs. Martin. "Yes, ma'am." Then she mouthed at me, "See what I mean?"

Things were no better a few nights later when Mr. Markoff asked some of us to remain after class. "Mrs. Martin has an interesting project up her sleeve," he said, and then went off to answer the phone.

At least Summer was one of the kids asked to stay. So was I. Also Rosemary, Clarence, Simon, and Peter. Peter and I squeezed each other's hands. Unfortunately, Meredith was staying, too. But not Jason. No wonder Summer backed against one of the pillars, crossed her arms, and pouted.

"Thank you for remaining," Mrs. Martin said, giving us the same glittering smile she used to charm parents with on Open House Nights back at Eastside Elementary. Seconds later, she turned to glare at a crowd of kids watching from the doorway. They hadn't been asked to stay. Jason stood at the very front of the group. His chin jutted. His eyes burned. His whole rigid stance challenged Mrs. Martin but she appeared not to notice. With a flick of her wrist, she shooed all the kids away.

"No spectators. And shut the door behind you."

After they were gone, she went on talking. "I've asked you seven to remain because I want you in a ballet I'm choreographing for our annual school demonstration."

Peter hugged me against him and whispered, "All right!"

"The demonstration takes place at the beginning of April," Mrs. Martin said. "Until then, besides continuing your regular classes, you will be rehearsing two or three evenings a week. Also on Saturday afternoons. Even Sundays. First rehearsal is next Saturday at one pm sharp. Any questions?"

I didn't have any. Like the others, I was flattered that she considered me good enough to be in her ballet. Shouldn't that prove to Mom that I had talent? To Apa, too? Also, being in the performance would give me needed stage experience. And the cherry on my sundae, of course, was to dance with Peter. I just hoped my folks would let me be in the ballet.

Still propped against the pillar, Summer waved a hand above her head. "One question, Ms. Martin, ma'am. Just exactly why did you choose us and not others?"

"Because most of you are capable of near-professional performances," Mrs. Martin said coolly, her face a mask. "All of you work hard. Also you fit specific roles I have in mind."

"What I'm getting at," Summer said, "is why am I the only black kid in this ballet."

"Because it requires that there be one black dancer and the rest white," Mrs. Martin said, then glided toward the door.

"Wait up, Stephanie," Summer said, plunging after her. "I don't buy that! What I'm asking, and you know it, is how come Jason isn't in your ballet."

Mrs. Martin spun and faced Summer. "I just told you. There is only one black role."

"The real reason, Stephanie, the real reason!"

"That is the real reason, one very real reason. But since you insist on having things spelled out, another is that I want you to concentrate on your role. Not on Jason Duval. I'm doing this ballet to show you off."

"At a ballet school demonstration? Oh,

give me a break!" Summer howled. "Just who'll see us except a bunch of parents and friends?"

"The man from New York will see you," Mrs. Martin snapped. "I have persuaded him to stop by a second time. And I don't want you or Lara or anyone else blowing it again."

I caught in my breath! This time I would show everybody I had talent. Including Mom.

Peter laced his fingers through mine. "Hey, could be we'll be going to New York together," he whispered. "That I wouldn't mind at all!"

I beamed at him, stroked the golden fuzz on his forearm, and tried to follow Summer's advice about letting him know how much I liked him.

He must have gotten the picture. After Mrs. Martin dismissed us, he took my hand and pulled me along the hall and into the small back room.

There, without a word and without switching on the lights, he grabbed me in his arms and started kissing me. His mouth nipped and sucked at mine, then, good grief, his tongue pushed inside. I stiffened for a second, then my whole body sort of dissolved.

Suddenly, the door swung open, the lights flashed on, and there stood Summer. I was both relieved and disappointed that she had come.

"Okay, you two, break it up," Summer said. "Stephanie's waiting to take Lara home."

An hour later in our front room, I didn't, of course, mention Peter, but I blurted out the news about Mrs. Martin's ballet and the man coming out from New York again. Standing near Apa's chair, I chewed my hair and waited for my folks' reaction.

"So you have another chance, little one," Apa said.

"It just means more time wasted," Mom said. "How'll you do your school work?"

"She'll do it, Liska," Apa said. "Doesn't she always?"

Mom grunted but made no more objections. So next Saturday, right after advanced class, I was waiting at the barre with the other kids for the first rehearsal to begin.

"The Black Goddess cometh," Summer said, sneering when Stephanie Martin swept in. And she did look like a goddess. Tall and haughty, she was as cold and expressionless as some of her ebony statues.

"What's up?" I asked Summer. "Are you still grounded?"

"Forever, now. Stephanie caught me sneaking out of my room and over the patio wall last night to meet Jason."

"Oh, wow!" I looked at Mrs. Martin sitting cross-legged on the floor. She pressed her back against a pillar. She gave off a faint fragrance of vanilla. Her long hands waved us down into a half-circle facing her. Her full-length practice skirt draped across her bare legs. They were the same rich brown as the floor. Clinging to her breasts, her black scoop-necked leotard showed her pointed nipples.

I crossed my arms over my own small breasts and wished mine were as full as hers, but the other night, kissing Peter, I had felt as if they were.

Next to me now he ran his hand under the criss-crossed straps of my leotard and flashed me a quick smile. Meredith must have noticed. Her face reddened and she bumped along on her behind until she arrived next to Clarence. He sent Simon a scared, white-eyed look, then a little smile.

Peter grunted. "Those weirdos! They'd rather sit next to each other any day than next to any girl!"

"What they do doesn't bother me," I said. "Especially if you'll — if you'll sit next to me, Peter."

He grinned. "Hey, that's what ballet is all about, isn't it? Boys like me getting close to girls like you."

Smiling into each other's eyes, we squeezed hands.

"If I may have your attention, Peter and Lara," Mrs. Martin snapped. "I was pointing out that most of you here are blondes. Only Lara, Peter, and Summer aren't."

Meredith gave a stagey giggle. "What a funny, peculiar way to pick a cast, Mrs. Martin. By hair color. How come?"

Meredith fluttered her lashes first at Clarence, then Simon. Another smile passed between the boys.

"What's her problem?" Peter growled. "Actually coming on to them."

"Not really, she isn't," I said.

Stephanie Martin aimed THE LOOK at Meredith. "Color happens to be fundamental to this ballet. Except for Summer, everybody will be blonde. Peter and Lara are going to wear blonde wigs."

"Then why can't Jason?" Summer asked.

The hollows deepened beneath Mrs. Martin's cheek bones. "Summer, I refuse to discuss Jason with you anymore. He is not, can not, will not be in this ballet. Period. End of discussion."

Scowling, Summer ran a finger along the grain of one of the boards but didn't argue.

"Today, I'll teach the circle dances," Mrs. Martin continued. "Most of the ballet, however, is built around the constantly shifting patterns of three couples juxtaposed with Summer."

"Mind translating that into Standard English?" Summer asked, but Mrs. Martin ignored her and started barking orders. "Summer, you're to help me teach the circle dances, since we won't be rehearsing your role right now. You saw me working out the choreography at home."

Summer set her hands on her hips. "You don't need me! Those dances are just a lot of skipping around. Why can't I split?"

Mrs. Martin stood up and gave her long skirt an abrupt shake.

"Okay. Okay. I get the point," Summer said. Dragging herself off the floor, she sagged against the barre. She reminded me of my rag doll.

"Now, everybody, on your feet," Mrs. Martin said. "Form a circle. No, not just any old way, Lara. Side by side with your partner. Rosemary with Simon. Meredith with Clarence, Lara with Peter."

Me with Peter! I laughed out loud. Being partners would really bring us close!

"Isn't that terrific, Peter?"

He swung my hand. "Hey, you know it! We'll be a team. Like the other night," he added, his face turning red.

"You are a group of children playing," Mrs. Martin said. "Dancing traditional circle games. Singing them, too. Only snatches. First, 'The Farmer in the Dell.' Join hands now and circle clockwise."

Clarence held one of my hands, Peter the other. Peter rubbed a finger along my palm until I felt like purring.

"Know what?" he whispered. "The way you like being stroked reminds me of a pussy cat. Think I'll call you that, pussy cat!"

"Clockwise, Lara!" Mrs. Martin yelled. I rushed to catch up.

"Now sway and slide," she went on. "But the slide is more of a glide, a *glissade*. No, Meredith, no! More naturally. This isn't classical ballet so don't turn your feet out."

Meredith giggled a little and tried to catch her partner's attention. "But kindergarten kids could do these steps, Mrs. Martin."

"Most of the ballet will be difficult enough even for you, sweetheart."

Meredith was being a real pain this afternoon, trying to act like she couldn't care less about losing Peter, I guess. When Mrs. Martin told us to sing "The Farmer in the Dell," Meredith asked, "How can we dance and sing at the same time? We won't have enough breath."

"Dancers do both in musicals all the time," Mrs. Martin said.

"Just ask Jason," Summer sang out from the barre. "He's been in lots of musicals. Should be in this ballet!"

Stephanie Martin didn't even look at Summer, just glared while the rest of us circled around and around. "Now change directions. The second game is one children play in Mexico. 'El Patio de mi Casa.' I'll sing it now but expect you to know the Spanish words for the next rehearsal."

Her low, vibrant voice filled the big studio. *"El patio de mi casa es particular."*

Peter whispered in my ear, *"Comprendes, chiquita?"*

"I didn't know you spoke Spanish," I said, surprised.

"I don't. I flunked it."

"You need to listen, Lara and Peter," Mrs. Martin snapped. "I said, when we come to the words, *chocolaté, chocolaté*, drop hands and clap. All right, from the beginning. And this time, try singing along with me in Spanish. That includes you, Lara!"

I bit my lip but didn't stay upset for long because I felt Peter's warm fingers on the back of my neck. I tingled all over. "Your topknot's coming down," he whispered.

"Why can't we just do all the games in English?" Meredith was asking.

Mrs. Martin's jaw tightened. "I put in the Mexican game because the ballet is international. If you prefer, we can use a French or German game. Even a game from Hungary if Lara can spare the time to show us one."

I hunched my shoulders. The mood Mrs. Martin was in, she might actually try to make me teach one. Why did she have to take it out on all of us just because she was mad at Summer?

"Or better yet, Lara, how about a folk dance?" Mrs. Martin went on. "The *csardas*, for instance. All Hungarians dance the *csardas*. Just as all black people eat side meat and greens," she added sarcastically. "So show us the *csardas*."

Peter pressed my hand but I felt tears coming anyway. "I — I don't know the *csardas*, Mrs. Martin. Really! Maybe my father does, but I've never even seen it."

"All right, Lara. All right. Just forget it." Mrs. Martin shifted her attention to Summer who was heading toward the door. "Exactly where do you think you are going?"

"Out," Summer said. "I'm splitting."

"You're staying right here," Mrs. Martin said.

Summer's chin went up. "And if I don't?"

"I believe we have already discussed consequences."

Shrugging, Summer slouched back to the barre. The rest of us did the Mexican game over and over until Mrs. Martin finally said, "All right, let's go on to 'Ring Around the Rosies.'"

Incredibly, Meredith giggled. "That baby stuff?"

"Hardly baby stuff, sweetheart," Mrs. Martin barked. " 'Ring Around the Rosies' originated in London during the plague. *Pocket full of posies* refers to flowers people carried around to sweeten the stench of hundreds of corpses."

I shuddered at the word *corpses*. Mom has told me about corpses left rotting all over Budapest during both World War II and the 1956 Revolution.

"Anyway, that's enough for this afternoon," Mrs. Martin said, then sighed. "You are all dismissed except Summer."

Summer, who was already halfway to the door, stopped. "Me? How come I have to stay?"

"Because we are going to work on your role."

"You said we weren't."

"I said, not while the others were here."

"But I've got plans, Stephanie."

"How can you? You're grounded. Especially after last night's little episode. We're going to work on your solo variation."

When Peter and I left Markoff's, instead of heading straight to the bus stop, we walked hand-in-hand to the ice cream parlor. Jason sat alone at a table near the window, obviously waiting for someone.

"Where's Summer?" he asked.

When I told him, he muttered, "Might have known! Dragon Lady's scared I'll mess up all her dreams for Summer. She's got dreams for Lara, too," he told Peter. "So take care, man, that she doesn't break up the two of you."

Chapter 13

We didn't rehearse again until after class on Wednesday night. The florescent lamps glared down. The air in the studio seemed damp and smelled of sweat. Still wearing our soggy practice clothes, we drooped against the barres. Meredith and Rosemary were yakking to Simon and Clarence. Peter turned his back on them and looped an arm around me.

Only Summer stood alone. Not for long, though! Jason bounced into the room and across to where she was sliding one leg along the barre to stretch her turn-out. He grabbed her from behind and started kissing her neck like they do in sexy movies.

Peter grinned at me. "Hey, I'll have to try that," he whispered, and did. I giggled and squirmed, but froze when, seconds later, Mrs. Martin whipped into the room. "What exactly is going on here?"

"Not a thing," Jason said. "Just giving my baby some lovin'."

"Get out!"

"Sure thing, Dragon Lady. See you later, Summer baby."

Silence. The silence continued while Jason sauntered out. Afterwards, too, until Mrs. Martin finally said, "I am a little bored with your immature behavior. I have tailored this ballet to show off what each of you does best, but I will have wasted my time unless you concentrate and learn your roles perfectly. So stop all the hanky-panky!"

My face burning, I detached myself from Peter and slid over beside Summer.

"Get her!" Summer muttered. "She must be forgetting how it was when she was our age and crazy about Blackbird."

"In this ballet you are young boys and girls playing," Mrs. Martin continued. "One pair is dreamy and gentle. The girl of the second couple is a clinging vine. The third two wrestle continuously."

"Which are Clarence and me, Mrs. Martin?" Meredith asked, blinking her pale lashes at him.

Peter growled, "Get her!"

"She doesn't mean anything, Peter," I said.

"You'll see when I show you," Stephanie Martin told Meredith.

"If I'd said Clarence and *me*," Summer whispered, "Stephanie would have yelled bloody murder about my awful grammar."

"And I would appreciate having your attention, Summer and Lara," Mrs. Martin snapped. "Summer, you are to teach Simon and Rosemary their variation."

"Yes, ma'am."

Summer led them to a corner while Mrs. Martin showed Clarence and Meredith some supported *pirouettes*. Clarence's partnering was strong. His technique was getting better and he showed promise of becoming a very good dancer. Peter and I watched, arm in arm. I was snuggling into the crook under his shoulder when Mrs. Martin shouted, "This is a rehearsal, Lara and Peter. Please pay attention even when I'm not working with you personally.

"Sorry," I faltered. Peter stammered something.

"Very well. Let us proceed. You two are the dreamy, innocent pair," she said dryly. "I've choreographed this variation especially for you, Lara. It's quite long and, if you do it well, it will show off your line and high extensions. First, *chaîné* to Peter. No, you must pull up!"

I heard the exasperation in her voice. Tears came to my eyes. I sucked in my waist and pulled up as hard as I could.

"Better," she said. "Now watch closely."

She showed us a long sequence of lovely supported turns and lifts. So lovely that, seeing her demonstrate them, I almost forgot to be nervous, especially since I would be dancing them with Peter. They were difficult, though, both the technique and the timing.

"Count, Lara, and pull up and jump. Jump, I said. Otherwise even a partner as strong as

125

Peter will have difficulty hoisting you."

I hung my head and pushed at my straggling hair. Then, all at once, I began to get the feel of the steps. When Peter lifted me through the *arabesque* jumps, one after another, I really sailed. The tiny flame in my chest flared and exploded through my body.

We worked on only the first half, but repeated it at least twenty times before Mrs. Martin said, "Okay, everybody, that's all for today. And, Peter and Lara, your variation may turn out to be quite nice if you two will just pay attention."

When she turned to talk to the other kids, Peter's lips brushed my ear. "Hey, it's really great dancing with you, pussy cat. Being close, I mean."

"Oh, yes," I murmured.

"You know where we're heading, don't you?" he asked and pulled me toward the hall.

"Wait a minute, Lara," Mrs. Martin called. "I want a private word with you, please. You may run along, Peter."

He strode off, shrugging. For several minutes Mrs. Martin regarded me silently. A frown pinched the smooth, dark skin between her eyes. "You know, Lara, we may make a dancer of you yet. Toward the end there you were really floating. I just wish you'd concentrate on Peter as a dancing partner and not as a male. Will you try?"

I nodded, but only to shut her up. Because for me Peter, the male and Peter, my dancing partner were the same man. Without him, I'd die. Probably not get to New York either.

The rest of the week we attended only our regular ballet classes, not any more practices. A good thing, too, because I was way behind on my homework. If I didn't watch out, the nuns would be sending notes home to my mother.

After Saturday's class, though, Mrs. Martin held another rehearsal. First, she had us put together everything we knew of the ballet so far. All except Summer. While the rest of us worked on our *pas de deux*, she pouted and slumped against the barre. The sun, shining through the bay window behind her, turned her into a silhouette.

"Next time, Summer," Mrs. Martin said, "you also are to dance. I've chalked an 'x' on the floor where your variation begins."

Summer ambled over to the mark and very slowly took her starting pose. Very slowly, too, her jaws started working on gum she had kept hidden till then.

"If dancing in this ballet is so boring, sweetheart," Mrs. Martin said in a tight voice, "I have two extremely talented black girls in my intermediate class. Either could easily replace you if I simplified the steps a little. I'm thinking of having them understudy the role anyway." Then she exploded. "Now get rid of that infernal gum!"

Summer strolled over to the door, took the gum between thumb and forefinger, looked at it, popped open her fingers, and let it fall. It clanked on the bottom of the metal waste basket.

Mrs. Martin turned away but her chest was heaving as if she had been dancing, too. "After the circle games and *pas de deux*," she panted, "the three couples do a *batterie* combination."

She walked through it, pantomiming the steps with her hands.

"First, dance in your line. Then girls repeat the combination going forward. Remember, there is no music until near the end of the ballet. I'll count for you now. Let's see it."

The tempo was so fast, so terribly fast, that I had to race to keep up.

"No, no, no!" Stephanie Martin shouted. She stopped us. "Stay in tempo. Everybody. Especially Lara."

I ducked my head, nearly starting to cry, but she didn't stop yelling. "It takes more than talent to become a dancer, Lara. If you expect even to go to New York, you must concentrate, concentrate, concentrate!"

Hunching my shoulders, I nodded. We went through the steps again. Then again. When we finished about the tenth run-through Mrs. Martin said, "Take five."

"About time!" Summer muttered, heading out to the drinking fountain.

Peter and I followed. When we arrived in the foyer, his arms went around me and I started to cry. "Sorry. Guess I'm really tired," I said, trying to sniff back my tears.

He laughed and squeezed me tighter in his big round arms. "Hey, it's okay. It's okay to cry on my shoulder. I'm your man, aren't I?"

I beamed at him through wet eyes. *My man!* Just like Jason was Summer's.

Summer looked up from the drinking fountain. Sunlight slanting through the leaded glass transom dyed her face red and green.

"So Peter's your man now, is he, girl? Terrific! But if Stephanie hears that, she'll give you the same lecture I got about Jason. Puppy love. Strictly glandular and won't last. Well, maybe her feelings for Blackbird didn't, but I know for sure that I don't want to go to New York or anywhere else without Jason."

Peter hugged me to his side. "Same goes for us, doesn't it, Lara?"

I nodded and blushed. I felt tingly and alive. I bent over the drinking fountain and was cooling my hot face in the arc of water when Meredith sauntered into the foyer.

"Mrs. Martin wonders where you all went. She says to get your butts back in there."

"I'll just bet she said that!" Peter growled.

I looked at him, surprised. I mean, they had just broken up, but why should her stupid remark make Peter so angry?

Her face turned red and she wet her lips. "Well, butts, fannies. What is it with you, Peter?" she asked, and fled through the door.

Shoulders tight, he stalked back to the studio on stiff legs.

Summer frowned. "What's going on?

"It seems to really bother him the way she's flirting with Simon and Clarence," I said.

She grinned. "Since Meredith went with Peter and now seems to be coming on to them, maybe he worries about being like them."

"But he's not. And what difference does it make anyway? They're both great guys, and they're terrific dancers."

"I know that, silly. Peter's just real mixed-up."

Arms folded, Mrs. Martin watched us scurry in. "If you two are quite ready, we'll get on with it. Remember to count."

She bent down and switched on the tape deck to a series of electronic sounds, followed by recorded rumbles of thunder. Remembering the storm during the audition last January, I shuddered.

We went through the variation once, then Stephanie Martin said, "Repeat the same thing, but now surround Summer."

When we finished the second time Mrs. Martin actually smiled. "Not too bad. Next, you're going to push Summer completely off stage."

We must have repeated the same dozen steps fifty times before the tape inside the cassette tangled. While Mrs. Martin fixed it, I sat on the piano bench to repin my torn *pointe* shoe ribbons. Peter knelt beside me. "Hey, Lara, if Mom'll let me borrow her car, what about going —"

But just then Meredith sidled up.

"What do you want?" Peter demanded.

"Heavens, I just want to let bygones be bygones. How do you like that so-called music? All the pings and whines. They grate on my nerves. Sounds like science fiction or something, don't you think, Peter?"

"How should I know?"

"My ballet is science fiction," Mrs. Martin called. "I adapted it from a short story by Ray Bradbury. It takes place in a classroom on Venus during the one day in every seven years that the sun shines there."

She stood up and frowned at the cassette in her hand.

"All the children were born on Venus except Margot, the role Summer is dancing."

"I. Am. Margot. Earth. Child," Summer said from the back of the room. Each word came out flat and separate. Arms jerking at right angles, she marched toward us.

"So far you're Margot," Stephanie Martin said. "But if your attitude doesn't improve.... Anyway, Margot came from Earth and is the only child who remembers the sun. This makes the Venus-born children jealous. So, to prevent her from seeing the sun today, they gang up and lock her in a closet."

Mrs. Martin arched an eyebrow like she used to when she was about to ask us a tricky question in fifth grade. "Does anyone happen to know what the story's called? No, not you,

Summer. You saw the title in the book at home."

Summer shrugged and sauntered back to the barre.

I remembered reading the story two years ago in ninth grade, but couldn't think of the name now.

"Never heard it before," Peter said.

"For shame, Peter. I thought you were a science fiction fan," Meredith said, wriggling and giggling. I frowned. She was sure coming on to him. If the two of them went to New York and I didn't, I was sure they would get back together, even if he did seem awfully hostile to her now.

"What makes you think I'm a science fiction fan?" Peter barked.

"Oh, well, I just thought you liked to read it, that's all." Meredith went to stand by Rosemary.

"No way. I never read anything except school stuff."

"Well, my mistake!" she said. "Pardon me. Then since I'm the only reader in the crowd, guess I'd better tell you all the answer. It's *All Summer in a Day.* Is that the name of the ballet, too, Mrs. Martin?"

"Yes, indeed, sweetheart!"

"Give the girl an A," Peter said sarcastically.

Meredith's face went red and her eyes got watery. I might have felt sorry for her but just then Peter hugged me, so all I could think of was how much I loved him.

Chapter 14

As the demonstration drew near, we rehearsed every day. We didn't only have to work on Stephanie Martin's ballet. We also had to go over and over the variations our class was going to dance.

After most rehearsals Peter and I spent time kissing and making out in the small studio.

"My mom would say it's positive reinforcement," he said one night, hurrying me down the hall, "except that we make out whether we've had a good rehearsal or not." He closed the door behind us and pulled me into his arms.

"But what if she knew we were doing this, Peter?" I asked, dodging his mouth. "I mean, wouldn't she think it was a sin? My mom certainly would."

"A sin? Doing these good things? She'd be all for it. So stop stalling, pussy cat."

He grabbed me in his arms and we started kissing. It was fantastic.

But the next time we went to the little room, the door was locked. A note thumbtacked at eye-level said, "THIS ROOM TO BE USED FOR SUPERVISED DANCE PRACTICE ONLY. KEY MAY BE SECURED FROM MR. MARKOFF OR MRS. MARTIN." It was signed in bold black script, *Stephanie Martin*.

On the morning of the demonstration, I took an early bus to the high school auditorium Mr. Markoff always rents for our performances. We had only rehearsed there a few times this year so I didn't know how I'd do on its unfamiliar stage. On the ride over I was so nervous that I went a couple of blocks too far and had to walk back. Doing well today not only meant going to New York, it meant going there with Peter.

My folks were coming later. Maybe Mom considers ballet a waste of time, but she never misses seeing me dance. Apa either, of course. This morning his eyes glittered and he was so excited he spilled his tea on Mom's clean tablecloth. You would think he was the one who was going to dance.

When I got to the auditorium, I found Summer already hanging onto a green property box and warming up.

"Girl," she said, poking a piece of gum into her mouth, "my butterflies are back by the horde. I'm not just ordinary every day nervous. I feel like an athlete, trying to decide whether to throw a game. If I dance okay and go to New York, I lose Jason be-

cause he's too old to try out for these scholarships. If I blow it, I lose my chance to go to
the Big Apple."

"I know how you feel."

"I doubt it. You'll go to New York. With
Peter! All you have to do is dance super good
today!"

"Oh, is that all!"

"You can do it, Lara. We both can. But I
don't want to if it means giving up Jason."

Other students began drifting in. Peter
arrived but instead of hugging me or anything, he just said hello and stood there. His
chest looked sort of caved in as if all the air
had been let out. His eyes had their vague,
clouded-over look.

"What's wrong, Peter?"

He lifted his shoulders. "Nothing. It's not
important."

"Tell me."

He gave another quick shrug. "Oh, well, I
just got a turn-down in the mail. Berkeley
doesn't want me at their great engineering
school. Not that I expected they would with
my grades. But Dad said to apply."

I brushed the fuzz on his forearm. "It
doesn't matter, Peter. You're going to New
York, remember?"

"That's what Mom said. 'Don't sweat it,'
she said. 'You only applied to please your
father.'"

I slipped my arm through his. "She's right,
Peter. Come on, do some *pliés* with me."

Grasping the make-shift barre, he lowered his knees in a *plié* but abruptly straightened them.

"There come those weirdos," he said, jerking his head towards Simon and Clarence. "This is all taken," he called to them.

"But there's room, Peter," I whispered.

"Not for them, there isn't."

I shook my head, frowning. "I don't understand," I said. "Why are you being like this?"

Peter's mouth tightened. He didn't answer, just glared at them. I was so embarrassed by Peter. I should have spoken up and asked them to sit down, but I was too worried about upsetting him. Clarence shrugged and they went away, smiling at each other.

Jason strolled in then. "How's it going, man?" he asked Peter. "Hi, baby!" he said to Summer. "You nervous or something, Lara?" he boomed to me. "You're looking paler than usual." Laughing hugely, he looked around, to make sure, I guess, that Stephanie Martin wasn't in sight, then started warming up next to Summer.

When Meredith came in, she began *pliés* in a corner by herself. She didn't speak even to Rosemary. Maybe her parents' coming today, a very unusual event, was making her nervous.

By the time Mr. Markoff arrived the entire advanced class was waiting. He tapped his gold-knobbed stick.

"Good morning. And it is a good morning.

Cold and bright outside. Inside, not a thing to worry about. Just concentrate and you'll all do beautifully. I'll keep the warm-up class brief because you will have to work without music this morning. Mr. Swensen is too ill to come."

"What's wrong?" Summer asked.

"Is he very sick?" I asked.

"Nothing serious. A touch of the flu. Fortunately, we're using taped music for the demonstration. All right, first position *pliés*."

After half an hour of warming our muscles, Mr. Markoff said, "Now go put on your make-up. Mrs. Martin went to the airport to meet Mr. Landon but asked me to remind you to stay in your assigned dressing rooms. Girls in the basement. Boys on the main floor."

"Wouldn't you know!" Summer said.

"Leave it to Dragon Lady," Jason said and followed Peter toward the men's dressing room.

When I reached the girls' dressing room, I looked behind me for Summer. She wasn't in the cold, low-ceilinged corridor or on the staircase. She hadn't arrived in the dressing room ahead of me, either. Only Rosemary was there, darkening her pale orange lashes with mascara.

"Well, at least you're here, Lara. Where is everybody?"

Before I could answer the door burst open and Meredith came in, panting. "Know where your friend Summer is, Lara?"

I shrugged and began tying one of Mom's old scarves around my head to keep makeup out of my hair.

"Well, maybe you're not interested, but Mrs. Martin sure will be," Meredith said, just as Mrs. Martin entered the dressing room.

"What will interest me?"

Meredith rolled her round blue eyes and tilted her chin at me. "Knowing where Summer is."

Mrs. Martin glanced around the room. "Obviously she isn't here, so where is she?"

"Oh, just behind the backdrop, making out with Jason Duval."

"I see," Mrs. Martin said quietly. "You may all start putting on your makeup. I will be back shortly."

"That was really creepy of you, Meredith," I said.

Smirking, she leaned toward the mirror and smeared pancake makeup all over her pointy face.

A few minutes later Mrs. Martin marched Summer into the room.

"You can let go my arm now," Summer said.

"All right, but you are to stay put. We'll discuss your behavior later. You already know the consequences. Now put on your makeup. Shadow your eyelids the way I showed you. And, Lara, use the black to outline your eyes. If you have big eyes, emphasize them!"

My hands were so cold and shaky that I wobbled the lines.

"Fifteen minutes," Mr. Markoff called from outside the door. "And, Stephanie, one of the crew has a question about your lighting."

"I'll be up in a minute," Mrs. Martin said. "Here, Lara, I'll help with the liner." But her hands were shaking as much as mine.

Handing the brush back to me, she gave a short laugh. "Do the best you can, all of you. Remember, regular leotards for your class exercises. No custom jobs. And bring your costumes for *All Summer* up to the wings now. I don't want you chasing downstairs to change following your class demonstration. I don't need to remind you, no talking in the wings. To anybody. Is that clear?" she asked, looking at Summer.

Summer only grunted and, after the others left, came over to me. "You ready, Lara?"

"I doubt it."

"Then pray a little. Put in a good word for me, too."

We got to the wings just as the beginners were finishing their dance. Skinny-legged, they rushed giggling off stage, nearly bumping into us. One little girl's wreath of plastic flowers dangled over her ear. She reminded me of Summer at our first demonstration five years ago.

"Sh-sh-sh!" came Mrs. Martin's hiss. "You little beginners go straight to your dressing room. And, Summer and Lara, you're blocking the wings. Please move away so my intermediates can get on stage."

She herded them past us and on stage. "If you forget the steps," she called after them, "follow the girl in front of you."

My stomach tightened. I couldn't remember a single step in either the class exercises or in my long *pas de deux* from Mrs. Martin's ballet. I hoped Peter did.

I saw him now, warming up on the other side of the stage. His legs, as beautiful and muscular as ever, were not bare and white today. For the demonstration, he had to wear tights like the rest of us.

"I said, we'd better do a few quick *pliés*, Lara," Summer said. Grasping arms to steady ourselves, we bent our knees several times. "Lord, my ribbons are cutting my ankles in two," Summer said, stopping.

She went up on *pointe* to test the tightness. Nearby, I heard a rumble of laughter. Looking around, I saw Jason lounging against a property box. He grinned at Summer seesawing from toe to toe.

"Watch out," she said. "Stephanie'll see you."

"Naw, baby. Right now she's got eyes for nobody but her little future Makarovas."

He was wrong. A minute later Stephanie Martin swooped down on Summer and Jason. She pointed a finger toward the second wing. "Go!" she told him. He shrugged and ambled off.

"And you, Summer Jones, are you willing

to throw away everything for that man? Going to the finals depends on how well you dance this afternoon. The same goes for you, Lara. Mr. Landon's plane was delayed, but he's finally here. Now get on stage. It's time for your class to dance."

By some miracle, I did okay in the combinations Mr. Markoff had choreographed for us. The steps seemed to come automatically, maybe because we performed all together or in small groups.

When my group wasn't dancing, I watched Peter from the wings. He skimmed along the floor, turned some nicely balanced *pirouettes*, remembered to point his toes and *plié*, but it wasn't his dancing that looked terrific, it was his body.

Jason's body wasn't bad, either. "Not bad atall," Summer whispered beside me in the wings. But it was his dancing that was really terrific. His air turns were startling. Almost as high and sure as Baryshnikov's. Why hadn't I noticed before? Maybe because Jason makes everything seem so easy.

When the class exercises ended, the cast of *All Summer in a Day* changed in the wings. My hands were so cold and sweaty I could hardly drag off my practice clothes and pull on my costume. It was supposed to be a space suit, iridescent orange tights with a matching long-sleeved leotard. It made me look seven feet tall!

All of us except Summer wore identical costumes. All were equally bright, only the colors were different. Summer pulled on a white tunic that showed off her dark skin.

"Places, please," Stephanie Martin called.

We started walking. It took forever to get out to the white x's she had chalked on the dark floor. A draft stirred through the auditorium. Shivering, I grasped my medal.

Please, Blessed Mother, help us all this afternoon.

Chapter 15

On stage we formed our circle. The blue gels snapped on. We began singing and dancing "The Farmer in the Dell." Downstage from us, Summer started turning *arabesques*. We were already circling in the blue light when the curtain sped up and clapping filled the dark auditorium.

We got through the games okay. Then came my *châiné* turns on *pointe*. I hoped the fake thunder and electronic noises would drown out the rapping of my *pointe* shoes on the floor. What I worried about most, though, were the lifts in the *pas de deux*.

I spun a series of turns toward Peter and, through my thin, slick leotard felt his hands grasp my waist. I unfolded my right leg high to the side, lowered it and formed a triangle against the other knee.

Staring into the black cave of the auditorium, I prayed I wouldn't slide off Peter's shoulder. I tightened my waist and jumped. Up I went, and perching on his hard, round muscles, I curved my arms above my head and shaped the sun.

Below me, Summer flickered her feet in a series of *brisés*, then spun *pirouettes* which gradually slowed and shifted into revolving, long-sustained *arabesques*. What incredible balance she had today! Her afro showed off her slender neck and gave her a wistful look, a tenderness.

When the thunder and lightning faded, Peter lowered me to the floor. We joined a mob of kids and pushed Summer into a closet where she wouldn't be able to see the great golden orb.

Soon the air brightened. The sun bloomed on the blue backdrop, a miraculous flower, a golden pomegranate. On the floor of the stage, a jungle of cardboard ferns sprouted. Now came bird twitters and flute trills from Rossini's *William Tell Overture*.

Peter grabbed me and we danced, then played hide-and-go-seek among the pale weeds in the spongy garden. While I was sprinting after him with high, stretched-out *grands jetés* and fast *arabesque* spins, the light in my chest ignited and flamed through my body.

Gradually, the air turned blue again. Thunder rumbled and lightning forked across the backdrop. We remembered Margot locked away in the closet and, after letting her out, watched her stretch her thin, dark arms toward the sun. But it was gone now and the storm had returned.

Afterward, we joined hands and like a ragged line of paper dolls, ran forward to bow to the audience. Parents and friends arrived backstage and collected in knots around their own dancer. I looked for the man from New York but didn't see him. Here came Mom, though, in the same black dress she wears to mass. Her thick braid circled her head like a crown.

Behind Mom limped Apa, wearing a new beret. His old suit was pressed and clean but in the glare of the stage's working lights, I could see where the cuffs were frayed. He hugged me.

"Beautiful, little one," he whispered. I hoped the man from New York would think so, too.

Mom said, "Yes, beautiful, but I never said you don't dance good, dear heart. I just said dancing ain't practical, don't bring in the bread and butter."

Apa laughed. "Did you ever hear that man does not live by bread alone, Liska? There is such a thing as food for the spirit. Which is what dancing and poetry are. They feed the soul and swell the heart. Good poetry and dance often have themes, too. Messages. The dance we just saw has one."

Mom's mouth drew into a knot. "My saints, something political, I spose. To you, what doesn't have?"

"Well, think about it, woman, and you'll see I'm right."

Sighing, I glanced quickly around the

stage. Still no man from New York. Peter had disappeared, too. Then I noticed people staring at my folks.

"Please don't argue here," I begged.

But Mom went right on. "Humph! Politics! If it wasn't for them political meetings you'd gone to, the AVH wouldn't of known you was in the fighting at all and we could of stayed in Hungary."

"Well, a man has to stand up for what he believes," Apa said. "For freedom. Or he isn't a man."

I looked around. People were still staring at my folks and, good grief, here came Stephanie Martin. But maybe she had news about New York.

"Good afternoon, Mrs. Havas, Mr. Havas," she said. "How nice of you to come. Wasn't Lara exquisite?"

My mouth dropped open. Exquisite! Me? Happiness bubbled through me. I even forgot to worry about New York.

Mom and Apa beamed.

"Did I hear you discussing my ballet?" Mrs. Martin asked.

"No," I said quickly.

"Yes," Apa said. "We were talking about what your ballet means. It's about freedom, I was telling my wife."

Mom lifted her chin. "And I say it's just a bunch of children being mean to little Summer and don't have nothing to do with politics or freedom or things like that."

I frowned and chewed a strand of hair

while Mrs. Martin gave them what in fifth grade we called her "keeping-the-peace" smile.

"Both of you are right. It is about children being children, but it is also about freedom. In the ballet the white children deprive the black child of hers."

Apa raised an eyebrow at Mom then went on discussing the ballet with Mrs. Martin. "It seems to me that your ballet is a little limited in its application, Mrs. Martin. Freedom is a world-wide problem. To gain it, people have come to this country for centuries just as my wife and I did. Doesn't the plaque on the State of Liberty say, 'Give me your tired, your poor, your huddled masses, yearning to breathe free'?"

My face grew hot but Mrs. Martin said, "Yes, you're quite right. And Ray Bradbury's story can be interpreted much more broadly. In it, race is not important. Margot is white, blue-eyed, yellow-haired. The coloring of the other children is never mentioned."

"Good," Apa said. "Then the original story could apply to anybody. For instance," he added, smiling, "it could apply to the Turks or the Austrians or the Germans or the Russians taking away the Hungarians' freedom. I'm curious to know why you changed the story as you did."

Mrs. Martin smiled, too. "Let's just say, Mr. Havas, that I wanted to say something about the freedom of my own people. But to return to Lara, you should be proud of her.

She's very talented and will make it to New York. If not this time, then someday."

Mrs. Martin drifted off to talk to another family. Someday! But I had to go to New York now with Peter. I still didn't see him. Had he already gone home?

"Hear that, Liska?" Apa asked beside me. "Mrs. Martin thinks our little one has a lot of talent."

Mom sniffed. "That don't make it so. That woman wanted to be a dancer herself and couldn't. So instead she's trying to make dancers out of Lara and Summer. Though I got to say you danced real nice today, dear heart."

I hugged her. "Thanks, Mom!" Now if the man from New York just thought so, too. I didn't see him. Or Peter, either. I did see Summer, though.

"Let's go say hello to Summer and her family," I said, and guided my folks through the crowd.

"Nice to see you all again," Summer's mother said. She is five feet tall and about the same width. The first time I went to Summer's house, her mother came out on the front porch in a flowered tent of a dress. Dropping straight from the shoulders, it bulged over her huge breasts and stomach. Summer's little brothers and sisters had come peeking at me from behind the fort of their mama's skirts.

Tonight Summer's mother was packed into

a shiny black dress. Her broad hips, like huge, satin-covered hams, seemed to move separately when she stepped up to shake hands with Apa and Mom.

"Didn't they both dance good tonight? Summer and your girl? They going far. To Hollywood, maybe."

"No, Mama. Not Hollywood," Summer said. Her face was shiny with sweat and excitement, but soon it fell like a cake when you open the oven door too soon. "It's New York we're maybe going to."

Biting her thumbnail, she glanced around. Was she looking for the man from New York or Jason? I didn't see either of them but someone was tugging on my hand.

"Shake hands with me, Lara. I 'member you," said Damone, Summer's sturdy, seven-year-old half brother.

I remembered him, too, although the first time I saw him, he was still in diapers. I had coaxed him out from behind his mother to shake my hand.

Same thing with Marvessa. Barely walking then, she must now be in second or third grade. Her hair was fixed in a hundred tiny beaded braids. She giggled and showed the same gap between her two front teeth that Summer had before she wore braces.

Summer pushed her other half sister forward. Tessie is taller, darker, actually prettier than Summer, but doesn't have Summer's liveliness.

"Tessie made the high school honor society again," Summer said. "That's four times in a row. She's going to be a doctor."

Ricky, Summer's full brother, is a year older than she and has the same light skin and eyes. Their father, like Steve, died in Vietnam.

"You remember my stepdaddy," Summer said. The towering black man reached out to shake hands with each of us in turn. I remembered how scared I was of him that first afternoon.

He had been working nights and sleeping days. Summer and I and the kids were playing a noisy game of tag around their big, shaggy couch when suddenly I looked up. There stood this giant who had to duck his head to get through the doorway. He had come out of the bedroom, barefooted and in jeans so short they showed his long ankle bones. Shaking hands with him then had been like shaking hands with a wrench. It was no different now.

"How do you do, Mr. Harris," I said to him just as Peter and his mother joined our group.

"Darling, here's Lara," she said to Peter. "The two of you danced so beautifully together."

He grinned and looked into my eyes. "Hey, we sure did!"

Blushing, I introduced them around the circle. His mother pumped every hand, then turned to my folks. "I'm sure you are proud to have such a talented daughter. Summer was good, too," she added, smiling at Summer's parents. "Neither of them can fail to make it to New York."

"We are very proud of Lara," my father said. "If they ask her to go to New York, we will be happy, but if they don't, we will be just as happy."

Mom nodded. "That's right."

Peter's arm went around my waist.

"You see," he whispered, "You did good, pussy cat!"

I giggled until I realized that my folks were staring at me, no doubt amazed to see Peter's arm around my waist. I pushed him away and stooped to tuck in a straggling *pointe* shoe ribbon.

When I stood up again, Peter was following his mother through the wings. He didn't even turn around to wave good-bye. How I must have hurt his feelings! Tears flooded my eyes.

Chapter 16

"Don't worry about Peter," Summer said after the stage door closed behind him. "Some ways he's pretty messed up, but I think he really likes you, Lara. Come on, let's go change."

"Might as well," I said. "Down there not as many people will see us bawl if we find out we didn't make it."

"Lord, you're such a pessimist!"

I turned to tell my folks I would meet them at the van and then trailed after Summer.

"Hurry up," she said.

"What's the big rush?"

But I saw. Jason was relaxing against a property box, his arms folded across his chest, his right instep draped across his left foot. He was smiling, of course. When isn't he?

Summer ran to him. "Come meet Mama now, Jason. You promised. Then come on home to supper with us."

He kept on smiling but said, "Naw, baby.

Like I said before, I got bad vibes about your mama."

Taking his hand, Summer tried to drag him toward her mother. "Please, Jason, Mama's nothing like Stephanie. She's sure to like you."

He shrugged and sauntered after her.

Summer's mother stood alone now. Her kids were romping up and down the auditorium. Her husband was off in the men's room.

"Mama, this is Jason Duval."

Summer's face followed Jason's like a sunflower follows the sun, so she didn't see the storm gathering on her mother's face.

"Jason's coming home to supper. He's the friend I told you about."

"Well, Mrs. Martin done told me about him, too," her mother snapped. "All about the both of you."

Jason shrugged and sort of slid away.

Hands on hips, Summer stuck out her lower lip.

"Mama, that's not fair! Believing Stephanie instead of me."

"Mrs. Martin knows what's best for you, girl."

Summer whirled away. "If Jason can't come home to supper, then I'm not coming, either! Let's go get dressed, Lara."

Her mother grabbed Summer by the arm. "You is too coming to supper. So're the Martins. Now go get yourself dressed, then back up these here stairs. Quick."

Hissing something under her breath, Summer stormed ahead of me down to the dressing room. She slammed herself onto a chair and smeared baby oil on her face.

Meredith sat slumped over the dressing table, dabbing her eyes with a Kleenex. I couldn't tell if she was blotting away eye makeup or tears. I didn't really care.

"Bad news about New York?" she asked Summer.

"Don't you wish!"

Meredith sat up straight and stared at us. "Then you really are going?"

"We haven't heard yet, Meredith honey," Summer said.

"Well, don't hold your breaths. Just because all your friends and relations came today and gushed about what divine dancers you are doesn't make it so. Even Rosemary's family came and she can't even turn a decent *pirouette*."

Her voice caught and tears shone in her eyes. I frowned.

"Didn't your folks come?" I asked. "I thought they were going to."

"At the last minute they had to leave town. Wouldn't you know? Some business emergency, they said."

"I'm really sorry, Meredith," I said.

She shrugged. "Don't be. I don't care. I'm going to New York and nobody else is. Except Peter. So we'll be there together, Lara, whether you like it or not."

Meredith is sort of like the alley cat I put milk out for on our back steps. Sometimes I think he wants to be friendly, but every time I start to get near, out shoot those claws.

"And even if you do make it to New York second time round," Meredith added, "it'll be all because of Stephanie Martin's friendly persuasion!"

"Did I hear my name taken in vain?" Mrs. Martin asked in the doorway. Silence. She came in, closed the door, and leaned against it.

"Oh, hello, Mrs. Martin," Meredith said, and went right on stuffing clothes into her satchel. "I was just saying what a great choreographer you are. Got to go now, though. Can't keep dear, faithful Mrs. Mueller waiting forever. She did show up. It's her job!"

After Meredith left, Mrs. Martin laughed. "I gather that whatever Meredith said wasn't particularly complimentary."

"Is it ever?" Summer asked.

"Hardly ever."

Then Mrs. Martin turned to me. "Lara, I want to talk to you first."

My stomach cramped. Here it came! I caught Summer's glance in the mirror and knew she was thinking the same thing.

"As I told your parents, Lara, your dancing this afternoon was exquisite. And strong! What's more, you projected your role beautifully."

"Uh, thanks." I coiled a piece of hair around a finger. Was she talking just to let me down easy?

"So spit it out," Summer said. "Did Lara make it or not?"

"I don't know yet if either of you have made it," Mrs. Martin said. "Mr. Markoff and Mr. Landon are still deciding. But I'm talking to Lara now. Not you."

"Figures!" Summer hunched over the dressing table and went on wiping off her makeup.

"Lara, your performance today showed great potential. I think you have the ability to develop into a classical ballerina perhaps as fine as your favorite, Cynthia Gregory. Of course, even to approach her technical prowess, not to mention her magnificent stage presence, you will have to work very, very hard and concentrate."

Her praise flooded me with happiness; then she added, "You cannot allow anything or anybody to distract you."

Anybody meant Peter. I sighed.

"But there is a more immediate problem, Lara. If you are invited to the finals in New York, will your parents let you go?"

"I'm sure my father will. I think maybe Mom will, too."

"If it's only a matter of the airfare, I'll be happy to loan you the money. But," she said, laughing a little, "we don't even know if you'll be asked to go, do we? And now I have some things to say to Summer."

Summer rolled her eyes and stuck out her lower lip. "Like what?"

"Like your dancing, for one thing, sweetheart. Today it was amazing. It showed that you are an extremely versatile dancer. Lyrical as well as allegro. Which Mr. Landon must have noticed. You have so much talent, it's frightening. And I don't want you to waste it."

"Who's wasting it?" Summer asked.

"You are. Now I want you to listen and listen carefully. A few minutes ago I found Jason Duval loitering at the top of the stairs, obviously waiting for you. And after what I told him, when I found you together behind the backdrop. So I dismissed him."

Summer jumped up. "You what? What do you mean, you dismissed him?"

"I mean, I told him that he may no longer study at Markoff's. May no longer take classes there."

"How could you? I'll talk to —"

Mrs. Martin gestured for silence. "I also told him that he's to move out of the house immediately. Find somewhere else to live."

Summer planted herself in front of Mrs. Martin. "I'll just talk to Mr. Markoff about this. He thinks Jason has a lot of talent."

Mrs. Martin crossed her arms and hollowed her cheeks. "Mr. Markoff and I have been watching this involvement of yours very carefully, Summer, and agree that it is out of hand. He thinks Jason has talent, but there

is no doubt about yours! And I don't intend
to let this Jason ruin your chances."

Summer's knees stiffened. "It won't work,
Stephanie," Summer said. "If Jason can't
come to Markoff's, I'll go wherever he goes."

"Are you willing to give up everything?"
Mrs. Martin demanded, nearly shouting.
"Your scholarship? Your chances of becoming a really good dancer — maybe even a
great dancer? Because those are the consequences."

I glanced at Summer's flaming face. A
great dancer? Yes, I thought, she could become one. And I wasn't jealous. All I cared
about was dancing, even if only in the *corps*.

But someone started knocking on the door.
I grasped my medal. Here came the news,
good or bad.

"That will be Mr. Markoff and the man
from New York," Mrs. Martin said, her voice
dropping back to its usual cool tone. "Come
in," she called.

In walked Mr. Markoff and Mr. Landon,
both smiling.

"Congratulations on your charming ballet,
Mrs. Martin," Mr. Landon said. "At the moment I can't remember its name, but I was
most impressed!" Then he took Summer and
me each by a hand. "And these two charming
girls. Dora and April?"

"Lara and Summer," Mrs. Martin said.

"Yes. Lara and Summer. Your performances were charming. And I must apologize.
Somehow in the stress of that stormy night

back in January I underestimated . . . or maybe you had off nights. But now I want you both in New York for the final audition later this month."

I squealed, jumped up, and hugged Summer. For a minute her face was as alive and happy as I felt. Then she slid down again, elbows on the table, chin in her palms. I knew what she was thinking. Going to New York meant leaving Jason. I didn't have that problem. Peter was coming with me. I just hoped he wasn't mad about me pushing him away tonight. Mrs. Martin and I thanked Mr. Landon, but Summer didn't say a word. She began packing her makeup into an old *pointe* shoe box.

"Summer, aren't you going to thank Mr. Landon?" Mrs. Martin asked. "He took a great deal of trouble to stop off in San José for a second look at you."

Summer rose slowly. "Yes, thanks a lot, Mr. Landon. It's just that. . . ."

"I quite understand," Mr. Landon said. "You're exhausted from all the rehearsals and extra practice sessions that Mrs. Martin's been putting you through. But I'm happy to return to right a wrong. Also to spot another extremely talented student."

"Oh?" Mrs. Martin asked.

"Yes. A dancer I don't remember seeing last January. He's over the age limit for our scholarship program but I've invited him to become an apprentice next fall. In the meantime, he will come to New York and start taking classes with the company immediately. Let's see, his name is John. Jack. James. Something like that."

Summer leaped up. Her eyes turned to stars. "Jason! It has to be Jason!"

"Jason Duval?" Mrs. Martin asked, glancing at Mr. Markoff. He shrugged.

"Yes. Yes. That's the one," Mr. Landon said. "Jason Duval. An exceptionally brilliant and powerful young dancer!"

Chapter 17

"I made it. I made it to New York!" I told Mom and Apa as soon as I got to the van.

Apa grinned. I could see why Mom accuses him of having gypsy eyes. They glinted at me, black and full of sparks. He crawled down from the driver's seat to hug me. By the stiff way he moved, I knew his arthritis was really hurting. Mom came down from her side, too, and put her arms around me.

"So you got what you wanted, dear heart," she said, sighing. "I'm glad except — except for you leaving us."

She gave me a weak little smile. Finally, she understood about my dancing. I hugged her. If I weren't worried about Peter being mad, I would be totally happy.

During the ride home, I sat on the wooden shelf Apa had built in the back of his van. It holds the soaps, solvents, polishes, and everything else he uses in his cleaning service.

Today a big, stringy mop kept flipping its smelly locks in my face. In fact, the whole van smelled. At first I was too excited to notice. Finally, I asked Apa if he would open his window a little. He did. The breeze was cold but blew away the stink. Every time we turned right, though, the mop still slapped me across the cheek. A memory slapped me, too. The hurt look in Peter's eyes.

When we got home, a beat-up old station wagon was taking up the curb space in front of our house. We have no garage because this neighborhood was built back in the days before a garage went with every house. Apa had to park half a block away and walk, which was really hard for him. Mom plodded ahead but I matched my steps to his.

When Apa and I reached the house, the whole place smelled of paprika. Hungarian stew for supper. Mom had already set the table. The red and green print of the cloth showed off her thick, shiny plates and some fragile old wine goblets she had bought years ago at a flea market.

"None of them match," she complained, "and they are thin as egg shells. They break if you so much as look at them." She is proud of them, though, and of the decanter, too, in spite of its chipped base. Today, sitting in the sun and filled with red tokay, it looked like a lighted red lantern.

"Fill the glasses, dear heart," Mom said. "Dancing good enough to go to New York is something to celebrate, I guess. Just wish it didn't mean you leaving home and not getting a proper education. But take your father his glass before he starts yelling for it."

The goblet was warm from sitting in the sun. I took it into the front room where Apa was reading. Looking up, his black eyes shimmered with pinpricks of light. He took the wine, and lifted the glass to me.

"To you, my little dancing Magyar."

He tossed down the tokay and handed the empty goblet back to me.

Golly, he must really be in a great mood. I had never seen him gulp wine that fast before.

He reached his hands to me. "Help me up, little one. I want to show you something."

Holding onto his thin wrists, I pulled him out of his chair. I couldn't believe what happened next! Usually, his arthritis pains him so much that some days he can hardly push a mop. Now he began limping in slow circles around our tiny front room. When he passed me, he snatched the empty goblet from my hand and shattered it against the lighted gas heater.

He laughed. "A fine custom but it needs a fireplace to do it right. Help me make more space in here."

Together we shoved Old Magyar beside the TV set.

"Watch closely now, daughter! I will dance for you as in the old days!"

By this time Mom had scuttled in from the kitchen. "What broke in here? Not my good wine glass, I hope. My saints, it was. How come? What's going on in here, Frank?"

He frowned. "This is between Lara and me, Liska," he said, turning his back on her.

He smiled at me, lifted his chest, arched his spine, and began humming a strange, slow tune. I had heard it before at the houses of Hungarian friends.

Keeping his arms pasted against his hips and thighs, Apa thrust his head and shoulders forward. His feet began creeping in long steps first to the right, then to the left. Slowly. Painfully.

Poor Apa reminded me of Giselle after the prince betrays her in the first act of the ballet Mrs. Martin took Summer and me to see last year. The girl goes crazy and wobbles through steps she used to perform lightly and beautifully. Apa's dance must be the ghost of one he did years ago in Hungary.

Now he changed tempo, shortened his steps, and tried to make them springy and fast. Instead, he staggered and limped. Suddenly, he stopped dead. Didn't move. Didn't hum. But his chest heaved and I heard his heavy breathing above the gasps of our ancient gas heater. He must be in terrible pain! Mom and I rushed to him, but he waved us back, me to my station beside the TV set, Mom to the kitchen doorway.

Gradually, he began moving again. He stretched out his arms, lifted his head, paced slowly. He wasn't humming anymore. Maybe he couldn't. Maybe he'd run out of breath. I saw how hard his chest was pumping. Then, slam, bang, feet drumming, actually shaking the floor, he spun crookedly around the room, a running-down top. Off flew his beret. His bald head gleamed.

What an incredible dance! It didn't matter that Apa's feet stumbled and dragged or that his arms waggled out to the sides like the arms of a scarecrow or the vanes of a broken windmill. His glittering eyes and the proud tilt of his head suggested a fierce beauty. The *csardas*! The dance had to be the *csardas*!

Its rhythm caught me, beat in my veins, in my temples, in my heart. The flame in my chest ignited and I found myself spinning after Apa faster and faster. I passed him by and kept whirling until I heard an awful crash behind me. I looked back and saw him sagging against the old chair. Its frame tilted crazily. Apa's eyes were spinning from all that turning. Maybe also from the wine.

I heard Mom muttering or maybe sobbing in the doorway. "Like a flame in the wind he was in them Budapest cafés," she said. "A flame in the wind."

She dabbed at her eyes with a corner of her apron. Her lips hung loose. She wiped her nose. For a second she was the thin bride in their blurry wedding snapshot taken on the steps of a church in Budapest. Narrow dress drooped to skinny ankles. Limp hat sagged over broad forehead. Long-stemmed daisies straggled from one hand.

"What got into you, Frank?" she cried. She grabbed him, pulled him against her and supported him to a straight chair near the kitchen door. "You trying to kill yourself or something? What made you do that fool dance?"

"Just an old Magyar who's had his hour," Apa growled. He moved a leg and winced. "I never really had my hour, though, did I, Liska? But now it's Lara's hour."

Mom sighed. "Just wish she'd stay here, Frank, and go to college. Become somebody."

"A dancer's somebody," Apa said. "A talented dancer is the best there is. And our Lara has lots of talent, plus a brave Magyar heart. Did you see how she danced the *csardas*? So she's going to New York and become somebody!"

Mom shrugged. "I'm wondering where she'll get the money from."

"If she wins a scholarship," Apa said quietly, "she will also receive what Mrs. Martin calls a 'living stipend.' The rest will come from Steve."

I caught my breath. Steve's precious money. Sacred. Like coins dropped into the boxes in front of holy shrines.

"Steve?" Mom cried.

Apa nodded. "Yes. His money will go to help Lara become a dancer. It will be like the scholarships rich people set up in memory of their dead children. It won't be as grand as I hear the Vietnam Veterans Memorial is in Washington, D.C., but it will be a living memorial to our son."

Tears came to my eyes. Mom started crying, too. She hugged me, but her voice caught. "That's for Lara's schooling, though, Frank. She's got to finish high school at least."

"Don't worry, Liska, she will. The scholarship doesn't begin until June so she can come back here and finish out the semester at St. Catherine's, and next fall start her senior year in New York. They have schools there, you know, Liska. Now help get me to the kitchen and we'll drink another toast to Lara's success."

"Seems to me you drunk a bit too many already," Mom said. But she poured more wine for everybody, then raised her glass to me.

"To you, dear heart, and your dancing, since that's what makes you happy."

Chapter 18

Right after we finished drinking the toast, the phone rang. Mom answered it. "For you, Lara. I think it's that big, nice-looking boy we met after you danced today."

I blushed.

"Well, you going to talk to him or not?" she asked. "You want me to say you don't want to?"

"No." But how could I talk to him in the middle of the kitchen. Grand Central Station!

I took the receiver, though, then held it while I waited for my folks to leave the room. Only they didn't. At the stove Mom lifted pan lids and pretended to sniff the goulash. At the table Apa frowned down at his newspaper and muttered in Hungarian.

I finally murmured a faint "hello" into the receiver.

"Hey, I can hardly hear you, pussy cat. It's Peter."

"Uh, hi."

"You sound funny. Your parents in the

room or something? Or are you mad about me hugging you in front of them this afternoon?"

"Of course not. I hope you aren't, either. But we're about to have supper so I can't talk now."

"Then I'll make it fast. Mom's letting me have the car and I'm wondering if I could come over."

I pressed one hand over the mouthpiece. "Uh, this boy Peter wants to know if he can come over."

Mom said, "Why, sure, dear heart. I been wondering how come you never bring home any boys. It's the natural thing for girls your age to do. More natural than spending all your time balleting. Tell him to come soon as we finish supper."

I couldn't believe it. After all my fears, Mom didn't mind if Peter came over. It was Apa who objected. He mumbled a stream of Hungarian too harsh and fast for me to understand.

"Now, Frank, calm down. His arm around her didn't mean nothing."

I caught my breath. They would never let Peter come.

Apa rapped the table so hard that the glasses and silverware sang.

"How would you know what it means, woman?" he snapped in English this time. "Lara is too young for boys to be coming around."

"She's sixteen. My saints, that's how old I was when we got married!"

Apa's face turned red. "Married!" he roared.

"Now, Frank, he's just coming to see her and maybe take her to a movie or something. Don't you remember Steve done that a couple of times in high school? Dating, they call it."

"Uh, what shall I tell Peter?" I asked, sucking an end of my hair.

"Why, tell him to come, dear heart," Mom said.

Apa grunted. "All right. All right. Only don't blame me."

"It's okay, Peter," I said, but I wondered if it was. My hands were shaky and cold.

Two hours later the doorbell rang.

"That was the bell, Lara," Mom called. She came pattering to my room where I was dashing a comb through my hair and wondering if green eyeliner would go okay with my jeans and red sweatshirt. I was afraid she would hassle me about the mess on my floor, but she seemed too excited to notice.

"My little girl's first boyfriend," she said, smiling in the doorway. Her eyes dreamed. "Frank was my first boyfriend, too. My only boyfriend." She glanced at me sideways. One corner of her mouth flipped up in a quick grin.

"We're only friends, Mom," I said, but my jumpy heart told me otherwise.

"My saints," Mom said, "you're not planning on wearing them raggedy jeans, are you, dear heart? What about that new plaid skirt I made you with the sweet, lacy little blouse?"

"Mom, we're not going anywhere. He's used to seeing me in jeans or practice clothes."

"Humph! Maybe that's why he ain't come here before!"

The door bell clanged again.

"Frank, you stuck in that chair or something? Answer the door."

"My arthritis hurts," Apa snapped. "Besides, he's not my friend."

"I'll get it then," Mom chirped and scrambled eagerly toward the door.

"Never mind. Never mind." I rushed past her, tossing my comb on top of the TV set just before I reached the front door.

Then I opened it and there under the amber porch lamp loomed Peter. The light turned his face golden, his eyes a clear yellow-green. Golly, his shoulders filled the entire doorway!

"Hi, Lara," he said, both hands sliding into his pockets.

I smiled up at him, hardly breathing, unable to say a word. He was so utterly gorgeous!

"Well, Lara, where's your manners?" Mom asked right behind me. "Ask your young man in."

My young man! I could have died! I slid out of the doorway. Peter edged inside and stood looking around him. The little room must have seemed bare to him. Nothing but Old Magyar, the gas heater, the TV, an orange-crate bookcase for Apa's volumes of poetry, and a couple of rickety straight chairs. If Peter sat on one of them, their toothpick legs might snap.

Mom beamed and shook Peter's hand. "Real nice to see you again."

Apa didn't even look up from his book. His scowl dragged his eyebrows so far over his eyes that I didn't know how he could read.

Mom glowered at Apa and cleared her throat. "Might as well come straight out to the kitchen," she chattered, bouncing ahead of Peter. "There's cabbage streusel left. A great, strong boy like you's usually hungry. I remember how Steve —" she began, then broke off. "Steve's our son, you know, that got killed in Vietnam."

Peter frowned and flashed me a question. "I didn't know," he said. "I'm sorry, Mrs. Havas."

I felt his eyes follow me to the kitchen table. Without meeting them, I sat down and motioned him to do the same. His huge, strong legs dwarfed the chair legs.

"Uh, go ahead and have some of Mom's famous streusel, Peter."

"Hey, that would be great," he said, but I could still feel him frowning. Mom set a huge slab of streusel in front of him.

"You having some, too?" she asked me.

I shook my head. The spicy goulash, good as it was, now sat like a huge, unchewed meatball in my stomach.

"That's our Lara," Mom said. "Eats like a bird. Wants to be a stick for this dancing. Not like you, so big and strong-looking."

I wound my legs around the chair legs and instead of looking at Peter, watched his fork carry big wedges of streusel to his mouth. Mom bustled about banging pans into cupboards, slamming drawers, scouring the sink, letting water roar from faucet to drain.

"Well, I got to excuse myself, go mend some of Lara's ballet tights," she finally said, and sort of tiptoed out of the kitchen. Thank heavens!

Peter looked up from his last bite and grinned, "Hey, your mother's kind of cute."

I ducked my head. "She really overdoes it."

"So does my mom. But she doesn't make great streusel like yours," he said, scraping his plate to scoop up the last of the thick sauce.

Finally I looked up and his eyes, cloudy green and troubled, met mine.

"Now what about this brother of yours who was killed in Nam? How come you never said anything about him, what with us being so close?"

Although I didn't really remember Steve, his trophies and baseball cards and his letter made me think I did. Sometimes I almost felt him moving about my room. Our room.

Tears came to my eyes. "I don't know, Peter. The subject just never came up. And it's, well, it's painful. Unfinished. A cut-off life. I can't explain. I know your dad was over there and everything, but he's regular Army. It's his job. Besides, he came back."

"Yeah. The conquering hero after sitting out the war in headquarters somewhere supervising the building of airstrips. Some hero!"

Peter's voice shook and his hands clenched into fists.

"But, Peter, I'm sure he had a hard time, did a good job and everything."

"Right! I'm sure."

Then his hands relaxed and he reached across the table and squeezed one of mine.

"So what about your brother? Steve? What did he do over in Nam?"

"Got killed," I blurted. I dabbed at my eyes with a paper napkin.

"Hey, don't cry. I just meant, was he in combat long. Maybe you have letters from him that tell what it was like."

"I've only read one of them."

"Maybe we could look at them. You know, read them together."

I shook my head. "Mom keeps them locked away. Besides, why would you want to read them? They're sad, really sad, especially when you know how soon everything was to end for him."

Peter sighed. "I know. I just thought I'd

like to see them, is all. Partly because he's your brother. Partly because —" He interrupted himself. "Hey, why don't you come over here and sit on my lap, pussy cat?"

He opened his arms and I slipped around the table and cuddled against him. We kissed a little, but could hear Mom and Apa muttering in the front room.

"Let's go out where we can talk. Where's that door go?" he asked, pointing to the kitchen door.

"To the backyard."

Peter reached for my hand. "Come on."

Our backyard isn't like the Martins'. No swimming pool, no chaise longues, no flower borders. Instead, there's Mom's withered vegetable garden, a leafless apricot tree, a clothes line between sagging posts, and the splintery gray back steps that have needed painting ever since my family moved here.

That's where we sat now, on the back stairs under a scattering of cold white stars.

Wrapping his arms around me, he pressed his warm cheek against mine, which was wet with tears.

"Cold, pussy cat?" he whispered.

I nodded and snuggled against his hard, warm chest. I felt slim and fragile in his firm arms. His jaw, a little prickly at the end of the day with beard, rubbed along my neck and cheek. He mouthed my ears and eyes and chin and finally my lips.

My heart drummed. Trembling, I grew

softer and softer until I was like melting butter. His big, warm hands slid up under my sweatshirt.

Suddenly, the back door slammed. Stairs and railing shook. On the porch above us, footsteps shuffled and scraped.

"I tell you, woman, they're out there somewhere in the dark and up to no good."

Peter and I leaped apart.

"My saints, Frank, let them be! Lara's a good girl brought up in the church. Besides, it's nice having a boy around again."

Chapter 19

During the weeks before we were to leave for New York, Peter came to my house practically every day. His mother was letting him drive her car to ballet. Afterwards he would take me home.

My mom glowed the minute he came in the door. She showered him with smiles and stuffed him with streusel. She was the happiest I had seen her since the Christmas my brother came home for the last time.

Once, when I returned from next door after borrowing milk for hot chocolate, I even found her showing Steve's letters to Peter.

For about a week following that first visit, my father didn't warm up to Peter at all. He would hardly even say hello. Then Apa found out Peter played chess. After that they had a game almost every time he came over.

"I haven't played this much since Steve went away," Apa told Peter one night, his eyes nearly hidden by his brows. "He was about your age when —" Apa broke off.

"I'm really sorry about your son, Mr. Havas."

His eyes watering, Apa nodded. "If only I felt his life hadn't been wasted."

Peter frowned. "People say it helps if you visit the Vietnam Veterans Memorial. Find your son's name there."

"In Washington, D.C.? I wish I could go."

"Hey, I have a great idea! Lara and I could go there for you. Take pictures of your son's name on the monument. We'll get Mrs. Martin to stop over after the audition. My dad lives in D.C. I suppose we could even stay with him."

"But how do you know Steve's name is even there?" I asked.

"It's got to be," Peter said. "The name of every serviceman and woman killed or missing in Vietnam is on the wall."

Next day, while I hung behind Peter, he mentioned his plan to Mrs. Martin.

"What about stopping in D.C. before instead of after the audition?" she asked. "My mother will be sixty years old the preceding Sunday and my brothers are pressuring me to come home for a party they're planning. She lives in Alexandria, just a few miles south of D.C."

"Hey, that would be great, wouldn't it, Lara?"

I nodded.

It's hard to believe how mellow Mrs. Martin has become since our ballet demonstration. Not only did she agree to the Washington trip, she hardly ever hassles me about Peter anymore. And she must realize we're together an awful lot at the studio and at my house and even on occasional real dates. Of course, she can't know how often we make out or how really far we go.

"I have to admit that Peter seems good for you, Lara," she said one night in the foyer after class. "Your dancing is much surer since you two have worked things out between you. But then he's not all flash and sweet talk," she added, aiming THE LOOK at Summer who had joined us.

"Guess that's a dig at Jason, huh, Stephanie? Could it maybe also apply to Blackbird? But, girl," Summer added, frowning at me, "take it easy with Peter. Don't get in over your head."

Mrs. Martin regarded me thoughtfully. "I'm sure, with your careful upbringing, Lara, you won't let yourself get carried away."

But the night before we were to leave for Washington and New York, she did intervene. Peter and I had planned a combination good-luck-in-New York, bon voyage, six-weeks-anniversary-since-we-made-up party.

We invited Summer along to dinner but she said, "No, seeing the two of you together would just make me even lonelier for Jason off in New York. Why couldn't he have waited and gone when we go instead of taking off with Mr. Landon right after the demonstration?"

By eight-thirty Peter and I had changed and were heading out the front door when Mrs. Martin stopped us. "Where do you two think you're going all dressed up?"

When we told her, she said, "Oh, no. Not tonight. I want you in bed and asleep by nine-thirty. You need to be well-rested for the trip. Not to mention for the audition. Absolutely no late partying until after next Friday. We won't even stay long at my mother's birthday party."

So Peter just drove me home. First, we stopped at MacDonald's, though. Then we parked near my house on a rise above the city and looked at all the lights strewn across the valley.

"See how pretty, Peter," I said, sitting forward and pointing through the steamed-up windshield. "Rows and rows of golden beads."

"Hey, pussy cat, you're sounding poetic tonight. Come here and let's make some poetry together."

I snuggled against the great swell of his chest. He unbuttoned my blouse and began kissing me. I felt so beautiful. But when he reached up under my skirt, I got scared. Scared about what Mom and the nuns would think. About what I'd have to say in confession. About what I felt was somehow missing in our friendship. It almost seemed as if only our bodies loved each other.

I sat up.

"We just can't, Peter."

"Hey, don't be like that, pussy cat."

His hands tried to drag me back against him, but I strained forward to the dashboard.

"I can't, Peter."

"Why not? We really like each other, don't we?"

"Yes, but I guess I don't feel ready yet."

"Well, uh, I brought rubbers, if you're afraid, you know, and aren't on the pill?"

I stared at him in the dim car. "The pill?" The word flew out of my throat like a scared sparrow.

"Well, yes. Meredith is."

"Meredith? How did she get into this?" I sort of shriveled. Now I knew for sure that Peter had had sex with her. How could he, when he claims to like me and seems not to like her at all?

"Cripes, Lara, I just mentioned her."

"Well, don't!" I was really crying now. Bawling.

He tried to pull me into his arms again, but I pressed myself against the door on my side of the front seat. The cold metal lever that opens the window shocked my skin. Sobbing, I buttoned and straightened my clothes.

"Awh, don't cry, Lara. Like I say, I like you a lot. I just wish I knew what's going on with you. I seem to really turn you on, then all of a sudden you don't want it."

Sobs clogged my throat so that I could

hardly talk. Tears streamed down my face. I started to hiccup.

"Don't be mad, Peter. It's not that I don't like you, it's just that I'm not ready to go all the way yet. Oh, I'm so mixed-up!"

I blinked out at the strings of lights in the valley. They shuddered and blurred through my tears.

"I — I guess you better take me home."

"I guess."

At my house, he wouldn't come in. I touched his arm. "Are you mad?"

"I just don't get it, that's all!"

After that disaster, hugging my rag doll, I went to bed and cried most of the night.

Next morning in the rush to leave, I tried to push aside my troubles with Peter. There was so much to do. So many new things happening. My first airplane ride. My first trip away from home. The visit to the Vietnam Memorial in Washington. The audition coming up. But at the front of my mind hung the worry that Peter would now go back to Meredith unless we could talk out our problems, work them out in New York.

On the ride to the airport, I sat in the back of the van as usual.

"Why so quiet?" Apa asked. His eyes glittered at me from the rear view mirror. "Our little Magyar's going to New York to be a dancer."

Mom peered around at me with big, wet

eyes. "To Washington, D.C., too. You'll be so far away, dear heart, so far."

As soon as we got to the airport, I glanced around for Peter. I didn't see him, but Summer ran up and hugged me.

"I got here super early so I'd have plenty of time to say good-bye to Mama and the kids. They're over there. Stephanie's off somewhere doing something about seat assignments. Daniel dropped us off on his way to work. You look pale, Lara. Got red eyes, too. Bet you're worried about your first plane ride. It's my first, too. We moved out here by car."

Even if there had been time, I don't know if I would have told her what was bothering me. But just then Mr. Markoff arrived. "Maybe I should spare you this," he said quietly, "but you would find out soon enough anyway. I'm sorry to say that Mr. Swensen died last night. Pneumonia."

"Oh, no!" My own worries sort of drained away. Summer and I sobbed against each other's shoulders.

Even Meredith cried a few tears. I turned my back on her, though. After what I had learned last night, I didn't want to look at her.

"Guess what, you nerds?" she said, with a toss of her blonde hair. "My parents are here. They're having coffee right now but they actually showed up to see me off, their daughter the ballerina!"

"Big deal," Summer said. I shrugged and looked around for Peter. It was getting late. A voice on the loudspeaker squawked boarding procedures. Mrs. Martin sped back from the airlines counter.

"Peter not here yet?" she asked. "I'll go phone his house."

When she returned, she said, "His mother says he's on his way."

I looked down the corridor past the security check station, but didn't see Peter. Now the loudspeaker blared the number of the row where our seats were assigned. The voice ordered us aboard. I hugged my folks.

"When you snap the picture of Steve's name, little one," Apa said, "remember not to stick your thumb over the lens."

"I won't, Apa."

"And, dear heart," Mom said. "Don't forget to light a candle for Steve at St. Patrick's."

"I won't, Mom." I hugged Apa again, then Mom, but all the time I was looking over their shoulders for Peter.

"All right, get aboard," Stephanie Martin said, nudging us toward the gate. "Go on, Summer. Meredith. You, too, Lara."

Just then I spotted Peter at the end of a line waiting to get through the security barricade. I started toward him but Mrs. Martin grabbed my arm. "Get on the plane, Lara!"

But I shook off Mrs. Martin's hand and ran down the corridor with her right behind me.

We got to the security station just as Peter walked through it. Bending over the conveyor belt, he picked up a strange-looking bundle sliding out of the curtained closet where they x-ray your luggage. The package was long and limp and wrapped in white freezer paper. It was the only thing he claimed. He must have checked his luggage at the airline ticket counter.

I ran into his arms and hugged him. At least, he didn't push me away! He was panting. He must have been running.

"I was afraid I'd be too late," he said.

"You are!" Mrs. Martin snapped. "I checked you in when I first arrived. So here's your boarding pass. Will you please get on the damn plane? Both of you."

Peter turned red and pushed one hand into his pocket. "Uh, I need to talk to Lara privately, Mrs. Martin."

I chewed a lock of hair. His voice cracked like maybe he was coming down with a cold. He wouldn't look at me. The long thin bundle quavered.

"It will have to wait," Mrs. Martin said. "You'll have five hours on the plane to talk before we arrive at Dulles International."

His legs stiffened. He straightened his back. "It's important, Mrs. Martin."

She looked up at the ceiling. "It always is with adolescents! All right, make it fast." She moved off a few steps. Peter led me to one of the big plate glass windows. Right outside, our plane was revving up.

"Uh, this is for you." He slipped the long bundle into my hands.

"What is it?" I asked, puzzled. Why couldn't he have given me this on the plane?

"Open it and find out." His lips were pale and tight. I still couldn't see his eyes. "Go ahead, open it."

Tearing off the wrapping, I found a single, long-stemmed red rose. My first flower. I pressed the waxy petals to my nose. They were wet with dew and too cold to be fragrant.

"Oh, Peter, how beautiful!"

"It's just from our yard. There weren't any flower shops open this early."

"That doesn't matter," I said. Then, suddenly, I stared at him. My voice shook. "I suppose — I suppose your mom picked it like she picked out Meredith's orchid."

He frowned. "No, Lara, I picked it myself. Really."

My heart soared. So he wasn't mad. Everything was all right. I smiled. "Oh, thanks a lot, Peter. But we'd better get on the plane."

He looked down and pocketed and unpocketed his hands.

"That's what I came to tell you, Lara. I'm not going."

I swayed. "What?" Maybe I hadn't heard him right. The jets outside the windows were making so much noise. The public address system was croaking, "Last call. Last call."

"What, Peter?" I asked again.

"I said, I'm not going."

I backed away. "But you can't not go." My voice rose to a wail. "You said last night you weren't mad."

"I'm not. You were right about us not being ready. But it shook me up. Then when I got home, I found two more turn-downs from colleges."

"But what does that matter? You don't need to go to college to be a dancer."

"That's just it. I'm not going to be a dancer. No talent. Only reason I got asked to New York is because I'm a man. Which my father doubts. He thinks you're only a man if you're straight."

"You know that's not true, Peter. You're a man — and so are Clarence and Simon."

"Well, my dad doesn't think so. When he found out last night about the colleges rejecting me, his voice got tight and sneering. I wanted to strangle him," Peter said.

He raised his hands, palms up, stared at them, clenched and unclenched them.

"My dad said, 'I suppose now you'll become a ballet dancer with the other queers.'"

Peter turned away, his great shoulders shaking. Sobs struggled out of his throat. I leaned my cheek against his arm.

"Peter, what does it matter what your father thinks? I know you're straight. So do you. And you're the one who's important."

"Yes, but I have to prove it to him. I just have to! Maybe to myself, too. So I'm enlisting tomorrow. Joining the Army."

"But what will that prove?" I yelled.

He shook his head. "Maybe if I get into combat like your brother. . . ."

"And killed like him?" I screamed. "You can't. You can't!"

I guess nobody heard me with the jet motors roaring and the loudspeaker squawking, "Last call for Passengers Havas, Manson, and Martin."

Next thing I knew Mrs. Martin was dragging me, and only me, through the cold morning air and over the trembling concrete to where the plane stood shuddering and ready to take off.

Chapter 20

I don't remember much about the plane ride. Only how cold my forehead got, pressing it against the icy double pane of the window. I stared down at the white froth that covered most of the country although it was the end of April. *Oh, Peter. Peter!*

When we arrived at Dulles International, Mrs. Martin herded us into the mouth of a tram that shuttles passengers directly from plane to terminal. Summer bounced ahead of us.

"Aren't these trams fantastic?" she asked.

"Haven't you ever been to Dulles before?" Meredith drawled. What a snot! Could be that she was missing Peter, too. Well, served her right!

"My, my," Summer crowed, plunking herself down on one of the tram's long benches, "so nice to have a world traveler along." She patted the place beside her. "Sit down here, Lara. Are you okay, girl?"

I saw Mrs. Martin's gaze swing to me and stick there.

I shrugged. "I'll live." But I felt so empty, as if all my insides had been scooped out.

Mrs. Martin rented a small car and we left Dulles and headed along what they call the Beltway. Like a huge wheel, it circles Washington, D.C.

"Wow, look at all the trees," Summer said. "I can just imagine Indians pattering through that forest on little moccasined feet, can't you, Lara?"

I looked out at the trees. After living in golden-brown California all my life, I noticed how green things were here. But the green reminded me of Peter's eyes, so I stopped looking.

When we approached a wide stretch of shining blue water, Meredith said, "That's the Potomac, the river the British sailed up when they burned Washington."

"And that was Alexandria we just passed," Mrs. Martin said. "I should have taken the last exit. Damn! We're going to be late to my mother's birthday dinner."

She negotiated several off and on ramps and finally nosed into a parking space at a single-storied brown and white motel.

"How come we're staying here?" Meredith asked. "What about your mother's house or one of those big hotels in Crystal City?"

"I'm sorry to disappoint you, sweetheart," Mrs. Martin said, "but my mother's little house will be filled with my brothers and their families. This motel may not be fancy but it's only a few blocks from where she lives. We should be there this minute, but first a shower for everyone and a change into respectable clothes. That means NO JEANS!"

Half an hour later Mrs. Martin, in pearls and creamy white wool, stopped the rental car at the foot of a sweep of lawn. On its brow stood a small, two-story house, fronted by four large white pillars.

"This is it," Mrs. Martin said. "And may I remind you that my mother is a no-nonsense woman. So mind your manners. And your grammar," she added, giving Summer THE LOOK.

Summer groaned. "I thought this was supposed to be a party!"

We climbed a long walkway and then a short flight of steps to the porch. Its wooden floor looked freshly painted and, unlike our porch at home, did not creak when we crossed it. Before we could lift the big shiny brass knocker, a girl of about ten popped out the front door.

"Here's Aunt Stephanie," she called over her shoulder and was immediately surrounded by a dozen people. They moved aside for a large, gray-haired woman in a long, beltless blue dress.

"Must be Stephanie's mother," Summer whispered to me. "The matriarch! I feel like I should curtsy."

The woman, a heavier, older, Stephanie

Martin, had the same high cheek bones and straight back. Her burning gaze slid from face to face, then settled on her daughter.

"We have been expecting you for an hour, my dear," she boomed in a low, vibrant voice.

"The plane was late, Mama," Mrs. Martin said meekly in the first lie I had ever heard her tell.

"Well, at least you have finally arrived," the woman said, opening her arms and pulling Mrs. Martin against her great opera singer bosom.

Laughing, two tall, handsome men, obviously Mrs. Martin's brothers, moved in and hugged her. "Welcome home, Steph."

A pair of plump, dark women about Mrs. Martin's age leaned close together, whispering and watching.

"Daughters-in-law," Summer hissed.

Half a dozen children bounded among the adults, shrieking hello's until the old woman withered them with a glance exactly like Mrs. Martin's famous look.

"So these are the three girls you mentioned," she said. Her eyes scorched Meredith, Summer, and me. "Where's the boy?"

That would be Peter. My stomach jolted. For a moment I had forgotten him.

"He couldn't come, Mama," Stephanie said quickly.

"Well, you might have let me know. Never mind, I'll just remove his place from the table. Come along to the dining room, everybody. And since it is so late, Stephanie, you and the girls may wash up downstairs in the powder room. Then come right in to dinner."

Followed by her sons, daughters-in-law, and grandchildren, the woman swept down the short entry hall.

"And you think I'm a dragon!" Mrs. Martin said.

"No wonder you ran off with Blackbird," Summer said, and received THE LOOK.

"None of that! Come wash your hands. And don't tell me they aren't dirty. Orders are orders in this house."

We crowded behind Mrs. Martin into a small white bathroom, rinsed our hands, dried them on tiny embroidered towels, and headed for the dining room.

Ten of us sat down to dinner under a gleaming, jangling chandelier that covered most of the ceiling and threatened to pull it down. The younger children overflowed to a card table set under the windows. There, away from the old woman's smoldering eyes, they chattered and giggled through the meal.

Course after course, beginning with a creamy soup, was served by the daughters-in-law.

When Mrs. Martin rose to help clear away the soup bowls, her mother roared, "Sit still, Stephanie. You are a guest. Besides, you never were much help in the kitchen."

"Lord," Summer whispered to me at the table, "I would have run away, too, with or without Blackbird!"

A discussion about local politics shunted between the brothers and their mother, but the rest of us, including Mrs. Martin, hardly said anything. We sang "Happy Birthday" when a cake flaming with sixty candles was settled in front of the old woman. But, instead of blowing out the blaze, she picked that moment to peer down the table at Summer.

"My daughter has kept me informed of your excellent progress, Summer Jones. I am not speaking about your dancing but about your development from a ghetto urchin using ghetto English to the mannerly child you are today."

The room went silent. Even the children at the card table stopped chattering and stared at Summer. The brothers gazed at her, their mouths twitching almost into smiles. Mrs. Martin's cheeks hollowed and her jaw tightened. I held my breath.

"Well, child, have you nothing to say?" asked the matriarch.

Her eyes turning golden, Summer bobbed her head politely. "Thank you very much, ma'm. I am very grateful for all that your daughter has done for me."

I bit my lips to keep from giggling. Mrs. Martin smiled and her face relaxed.

Her mother said, "I am happy you are so appreciative, Summer. I'm afraid my own children were less so. Especially Stephanie, but she finally straightened out. You must understand that, although I worked and brought up three children alone, I insisted that they speak correct English. Except, of course, occasionally among themselves."

She aimed a surprisingly beautiful young smile at her sons.

"Right on, Mama!" one of them said. "Now blow out your candles."

Soon after dinner, Mrs. Martin kissed her mother. "The girls are exhausted from the long flight, Mama, so I'm afraid we will have to say good-night."

The brothers accompanied us down the long walk to the car.

"You see, Steph, it wasn't so bad, now was it?" one of them asked.

Mrs. Martin laughed a little. "At least she didn't send me to bed with no supper for using a double negative. And you, Summer, deserve a medal for your performance. Thanks."

"That's okay, Stephanie. You owe me one."

Next morning, on the advice of Mrs. Martin's brother, we left the rental car at the motel and caught one of the bright new Metro trains.

"How come we're traveling out in the open?" Summer asked. "I thought subways were supposed to be underground."

Later our train dived underground. We were in a dark tunnel when the operator announced, "Next stop, The Pentagon." I shuddered. One of those crisply-uniformed officers getting off might be Peter's father.

We stayed on the train as far as Archives station, then caught a bus to the Lincoln

Memorial. Standing with us on the steps, Mrs. Martin swept a hand toward the reflecting pool and long green lawns that stretched between us and the spearlike Washington Monument.

"That's the Mall," she said. "Today it's nearly deserted, but once in the early Sixties, when I was just a kid, I saw it jammed with freedom marchers led by Martin Luther King."

For a minute her eyes filmed over with a long-ago look, then she turned to us briskly. "I'm going to climb on up and say hello to Old Abe. Come along, Meredith," she added, apparently sensing a real need to separate Meredith and me. "You two go down to the Vietnam Memorial," she said to Summer and me.

We saw it first from across a sloping lawn, a long, dark gash like a wound in the grass. People in small groups or alone were walking down or up a slanting walkway that parallels a wall of polished black granite.

"We look up their names over there," Summer said, pointing to several glass-covered stands that resembled museum cases. "Here's one for you, Lara. I'll use the next one. Nobody's there now."

After she left, I stared through the protecting glass at a thick directory that looked like an ordinary telephone book. In it, names were listed alphabetically. I reached under the glass and flipped through the pages to 'H', then ran my finger down the gray print. Hartfield. Hartley. There it was! My heart stopped. Havas. Only one Havas. Then I stared. It wasn't Havas, Steve, as I expected. It was *Havas, István*. My brother must have registered under his Hungarian name. Tears flooded my eyes and blurred the page.

Summer touched my elbow. "I found my father," she whispered. "Did you find your brother?"

I nodded.

"What panel is he on?" she asked.

"Panel?" In the shock of finding him, I had only noticed his name. I looked again. *Havas, István. Pfc. 1 Jul 53. 10 Oct 72. San José CA 2W 80.* Pfc was his rank. Private First Class. The first date was his birthday. The second? Dear God, that was the day he died! San José was his hometown.

"But what are the numbers at the end?" I asked.

"The first one is the panel number, the second is the line his name is on. Don't you ever read instructions, girl? 'W' means West so he's on the second panel before the wall angles East. His name is eighty lines down from the top of the panel. My dad is on panel 53East. He was killed in 1968, same year I was born. I'll look for him after we find your brother."

"Thanks, Summer, but I want to find him myself. Is that okay?"

"Course," she said, and trotted off down the walk, the polished wall reflecting her slight figure in jeans and sweatshirt. It reflected mine, too, when I edged down the incline past the names of hundreds, thousands of Vietnam dead and missing. I watched for the numbers at the lower corners of the panels: 70W, 35W, 18W. Finally, I came to 2W and drew a shaky breath. Now to find the line. A dot marks every tenth row so, starting from the top, I counted by tens down to 80. Suddenly his name jumped out at me. *István Havas*. My brother!

To steady myself I held on to the narrow rope that cordons wall from walkway.

"May I help you find a name, miss?" asked a man in a wrinkled camouflage uniform. A shaggy beard hid his jaw. An orange band bound his long frizzy hair. "My name might have been on the wall, too," he went on, "but I came back, so I take turns here with some of my buddies to help people find the names of those they lost."

"Thanks, but I think I've found him."

"Great. If you have a camera, I'll take a picture of his name for you."

"Thanks, but I can do it." I dug into my purse and brought out the small camera Apa had lent me. Blinking through wet eyes, I leaned close and snapped the picture. I was through now but, staring into the black mirror, seeing my reflection across my brother's name, I couldn't seem to leave. If only there were some way to take more of this home to my folks.

"Would you like me to make you a rubbing of his name?" asked the shaggy veteran.

"What's a rubbing?"

"Got a pencil? You hold a piece of paper against the wall and scribble over the name. That way you'll have a real souvenir."

I smiled at him. "Thanks, but I'd like to do it myself."

I stepped over the cordon and onto the thin strip of grass that borders the wall. Out of my purse I took the green-and-white leaflet that explains the Memorial. Pressing it against the wall, I carefully zigzagged the pencil across my brother's name. Under my fingerprints, the smooth, sunlit wall burned hot. I removed the leaflet and saw, in clear white letters, my brother's proud and noble name, *István Havas*.

"Rest in peace," I murmured and, putting the rubbing in my purse to take home to my folks, I turned away to find Summer.

Chapter 21

When we arrived in New York the next day,
the weather was clear and cold. A wind blew
constantly from both rivers but mostly off
the Hudson. Mornings it pushed us along
from our hotel to classes at the ballet school.
Stephanie Martin was insisting we take them
so that we would be in top shape for the
audition on Friday.

The wind blew every afternoon, too. I
wanted to go back to the hotel after class and
climb under the covers but Mrs. Martin led
us through the windy streets to the United
Nations on Tuesday, to the Guggenheim on
Wednesday, and to the Frick Museum on
Thursday. There she gathered us in front of
a painting by Degas. Two stocky dancers and
parts of two others extended their right legs
in wobbly second positions.

"Would you just look at their feet!" Summer exclaimed. "They're rolling way over on
the insides of their arches. No way would

they make it through the audition tomorrow!"

Just seeing them made me shiver. Bare arms, bare shoulders, bare legs poked out of frilly, old-fashioned costumes. They must be freezing. Or was I the one who was cold? I buttoned my coat up to my neck.

In New York I seemed to be missing Peter more than I had in Washington. There, I had concentrated on finding my brother's name on the Veterans Memorial. In New York, however, I was spending a lot of time in the ballet studio and, since this one was not much different than Markoff's, I half expected to see Peter doing *pliés* across the room from me or feel his big arms going around me. Of course, Meredith was always right there in person!

As for my dancing, it was terrible. I couldn't manage a decent *pirouette*! I tripped on most of my beats and toppled off my *attitude* turns. I was limp as the rag doll on my bed at home.

"Pull yourself together, girl," Summer said one noon after class. "Losing Peter's not the end of the world. I miss Jason, too, but am I falling apart?"

I sniffed. "But Jason's just off in Puerto Rico with the company and will be back in New York any minute. Peter, I'll never see again. I can't seem to dance without him. Or don't want to."

Then, after all the windy, clear weather,

on the morning of the audition it started raining. I shivered looking through the hotel window and up a shaft between skyscrapers to a sky all draggy and gray with clouds. That's how I felt, too. Draggy and gray.

About noon we took the cramped elevator down and went out on the wet, gray sidewalk to coax a taxi to stop. Rain blew in our faces and seeped into my imitation Adidas. The bad weather was why Stephanie Martin was taking us to the ballet school in a cab. Also she wanted us there early. The traffic growled and honked past us. A taxi finally stopped.

"Get in, all of you," Mrs. Martin said.

I backed away. "I'd like to walk and stop by St. Patrick's, Mrs. Martin. I promised my mother."

"Can't that possibly wait till after the audition?"

"I'd like to go now, Mrs. Martin."

I felt Summer studying me. "Give Lara a break, Stephanie. Maybe she'll put in a good word for us this afternoon. Even you, Meredith!"

"All right, all right," Mrs. Martin said. "Only don't be late, Lara. Remember, the audition is at two pm sharp. The way you've been dancing this week . . ." she began, then shrugged. "Well, maybe a prayer will help. So might a thorough warm-up. Be at the studio by one at the very latest."

Hurrying away in case she changed her mind, I headed south. I had never been to St. Patrick's Cathedral, but Mom spent a lot of time there when she first came to the United States. From her description and from the postcard on her dresser, I recognized St. Patrick's as soon as I saw it. A mass of carved, ash-colored stone at the feet of looming buildings.

I pushed open one of the heavy doors and went inside. The familiar odor of candle wax and incense calmed me a little. I crossed myself with holy water from the marble font near the door, then followed Mom's directions exactly. Down the right hand aisle and past a dozen side altars. Finally, behind the main altar, I found what I was looking for, the chapel of Our Lady of Lourdes.

At the entrance I dropped a quarter into the lead box and heard it clank on the bottom. I set a creamy new candle in a little red cup, lit the wick, and knelt on the stony floor. Clasping my hands under my chin, I gazed at the figure of Our Lady of Lourdes. I pressed my medal against my chest.

Blessed Mother, hear my prayers.

I kept my promise to Mom and prayed for Steve. I also said a prayer for her and for Apa. I asked that his arthritis get better. Then I prayed for Mr. Swensen, who is dead now and no longer bothered by arthritis. "And Peter," I began, but didn't know what more to say so I just kept repeating his name. "Peter! Oh, Peter!"

I was about to ask for help in the audition when, behind my shoulder, I heard a muttering. Was somebody watching me? I looked around. Nobody. Nothing. Only the bank of fluttering candles. Tiny flames dipped and stretched in a breeze drifting through the cathedral.

I saw the candle I had lit. Its white tongue was fluttering, too. A flame in the wind, like Apa when he used to dance. Like he wanted me to dance. "Where's your Magyar spirit, little one?" I could almost hear him asking me.

I felt a spurt of energy, a dash of Hungarian paprika. Okay, so I detested Meredith and had lost Peter. I really missed him, but I couldn't let him or Meredith keep me from becoming a dancer. And since I was in New York to audition, I had better get over to the studio fast.

I pushed myself up from the floor and ran down an aisle and out a side door. In the rain again, I panicked. What time was it? Had the audition already started?

When I reached the ballet school, I stopped at the foot of the narrow staircase. I was out of breath and wet. I had run all the way from St. Patrick's without opening my umbrella.

That's when Summer appeared. She dashed down the staircase two steps at a time, a blur of pink tights and white leotard. Her jaws were working double time on a wad of gum.

"What the heck took you so long, Lara? It's nearly two o'clock! Stephanie's upstairs freaking out!"

Summer's thin, dark arms wrapped around me. Then she backed off. A frown puckered her forehead. Her eyes searched my face.

"Did going to St. Pat's help?"

"I think so. I miss Peter and don't understand about him and Meredith, but I have to be a dancer."

Summer frowned. "So you found out about them!"

I caught my breath. "You knew? Why didn't you tell me?"

"What did it matter? I didn't want to upset you. And if Meredith weren't such a creep I'd almost feel sorry for her. After all, Peter up and left her when he went back to you. But that's all ancient history now. You said Peter's joining the Army and you're going to be a dancer. So get upstairs. You've got to get your audition number. See, I already have mine. Fifteen. My precise age. Maybe it'll bring me luck!"

She stuck out her chest to show me the big fifteen on her leotard, and ran ahead of me up to the fourth floor landing. I trailed behind, biting my lips, but had more or less calmed down by the time I saw the black letters on a faded blue door that said: SCHOOL OF THE NEW YORK BALLET ASSOCIATION.

This was where we had been taking class all week. I followed Summer into the foyer. Today it was wall-to-wall dancers. I spotted Mrs. Martin leaning over the reception desk talking to the secretary.

"She's probably trying to persuade the woman to call out New York's finest to search for you," Summer said.

At that moment Mrs. Martin spotted us and started our way.

Summer grabbed me by the arm and pulled me into the dressing room.

"Lord, we can sure do without her reminders to turn out, to pull up, and not to wear custom leotards at this point in time, as Daniel would say. This is it!"

Summer chewed her gum fast. I stripped off my wet clothes, dried my face and hair, and changed into tights and leotard. My hands were so cold and shaky that it took me forever to pin up my topknot and to wrap, tie, and tuck in the ends of my *pointe* shoe ribbons. I stepped on toe and winced. My arches cramped. My feet drew up like crabs.

"Never mind," Summer said, "they'll relax as soon as we start. So will you, I hope. Now you've got to get your audition number. And I've got to get rid of this gum before Stephanie sees it and starts screaming. Come on."

"Okay," I said, but before following her, I gripped my medal and closed my eyes.

Help me, Holy Mother. Summer, too.

But I couldn't bring myself to include Meredith's name in my prayer.

Chapter 22

The dancers were funneling into the large
studio when Summer and I reached the foyer.

"Hurry, hurry," called a small, plump man
I recognized as Mr. Landon. "Go on in," he
told us, then stopped me. "Where's your
number, young lady? What's your name?
Were you at a preliminary audition?"

I couldn't believe it! Mr. Landon didn't
remember me!

"You know Lara," Summer said. "She's
from San José. Same as me."

"Oh, yes. But run along, Fifteen. I can
look up Lara's papers without your help."

"Is there a problem?" Stephanie Martin
asked, appearing from nowhere.

"Not really. This girl's papers must be
here somewhere. Yes, I've found them. Let's
see. Lara Havas. You're Thirty-one. Thirteen
backwards." He chuckled. "You aren't super-
stitious, are you? Go on in and find your slot
between Numbers Thirty and Thirty-two."

Stephanie Martin started to follow but Mr.

Landon called her back. "I'm sorry, Mrs. Martin, no observers. Only contestants. You'll have to wait out here with the other teachers and parents."

Inside the classroom, the contestants stood in rows according to number. I found my place between two boys. Sliding into line, I glanced first at one, then at the other. Number Thirty was short and small-boned. He looked about twelve. Number Thirty-two was older, about my height, and had dark brown eyes, not sea-green like Peter's.

Number Thirty-two grinned at me. "Hi!"

"Hi," I said quickly, feeling my face flush. I turned away and looked for Summer.

I saw her and Meredith in the second row. Summer waved, but creepy Meredith was too busy chattering with a boy next to her. Her number was Eighteen; his, Nineteen. What would Peter's have been? Frowning, I bent my knees in a deep *plié*.

Beside me, Number Thirty-two said, "See them at the table? Five executioners sitting in a row. They make me real nervous. How about you?"

Without meeting his eyes, I nodded and, after a glance at the table, turned toward the piano. If only Mr. Swensen sat there waiting to play. He would be smiling at me, not reading a paperback mystery like that young pianist with the black beard. The young man caught me staring and winked. Blushing, I looked out a window at the back of the room. The weather remained gloomy and gray. If only the sun would shine. Instead, rain began pelting the dusty glass and Mr. Landon bobbed into the room.

"Everyone should already have been screened, either during last Tuesday's audition here in New York or in earlier try-outs in various parts of the country," he said. "Everyone has? Good. Then line up at the barres by number. Higher numbers use the portables in the center, please."

I was one of the higher numbers. So were the boys beside me. Summer and Meredith took places at a regular barre fastened to the wall. At least this studio didn't have center pillars like the disastrous ones at Markoff's!

At the front of the room Mr. Landon clapped his hands and started class with *demi-pliés*. At the table the five judges began scribbling on their note pads. All during the audition they would jot down how our feet arched and pointed, whether our backs were strong and flexible, and if we turned out enough and from the hips.

Pressing my hand against the medal under my leotard, I asked for strength. I got through barre exercises.

Mr. Landon cleared his throat. "Thank you. The following are now excused." He called a list of numbers, but not those on each side of me. Not mine, either. Not this time.

"Hey, we survived the first cut!" whispered Number Thirty-two. I couldn't help smiling, although his cheerful "hey" reminded me of Peter. Two rows ahead of us Summer was waving. She had survived, too. Also Meredith, unfortunately.

I helped Numbers Thirty and Thirty-two move our portable barre out of the way to clear space for center floor exercises.

"Hey, ever consider becoming a furniture mover?" Number Thirty-two whispered, grinning. There was that "hey" again but I managed to smile, then wedged my feet into fifth position for the first adagio combination. *Concentrate*, I told myself. *Think balance!*

Standing on my left leg, I extended my right into a high first position *développé*, around to second, then back into *attitude*. When we finished the combination, I was positive that I had done well, but Mr. Landon said, "Let me caution you: wobbling cancels out even the highest extensions."

I caught in my breath. Could he mean me? Had I wobbled?

"Now the other side," he said.

I frowned. My left *développé* has been lower than my right ever since I strained a muscle in my groin last November. But inhaling deeply, I pulled up from the waist and managed the exercise on the left side.

After we finished, Mr. Landon talked to the judges. The black-bearded pianist used the pause to draw his mystery out of his back pocket and read. How could he be so callous and cold when this audition meant so much to so many? But the wink he sent me over his paperback was anything but cold. My face was still burning when Mr. Landon started calling numbers again.

"Actually," Number Thirty-two whispered, "they're lottery numbers and this is a human lottery."

The lottery caught Number Thirty that time. I watched the poor kid skulk out the door.

"Too close for comfort, huh?" Number Thirty-two muttered.

I nodded and looked for Summer. She was still in the competition. Meredith, too.

"*Pirouettes* next. Girls on *pointe*," Mr. Landon called and rattled off the names of steps he wanted. "Then turns from fifth position."

Fifth position *pirouettes.* We hadn't worked on them much in San José. Since the balance is different, I staggered a little coming off them. So did Summer, I noticed. But we both did all the turns. She looked back at me and mouthed, "We're fantastic!"

After *pirouettes*, Mr. Landon returned to the judges' table. Would he call my number now? I held my breath but this time he didn't eliminate anybody. Instead he asked for beats. I groaned softly.

"You don't like beats?" Number Thirty-two asked.

I shook my head.

"You'll do okay," he whispered.

And I did. Maybe my feet weren't as neat as his or Summer's or Meredith's, but I beat every *brisé*, every *entrechat*, every *royale* that Mr. Landon wanted. Afterwards, he read off more lottery numbers. Not Thirty-one, though, thank heavens.

Big jumps followed. We lined up in the corner by pairs and waited to dance diagonally across the room. With Summer as my partner, I almost felt as if I were back in San José. Just to be safe, though, I crossed myself.

"Tell yourself you're the greatest, Lara, like I do," she whispered. "Sometimes I almost believe it."

Ahead of us Number Thirty-two waited to begin the jumping combination with Number Nineteen, Meredith's new friend. Just before they sailed off, Number Thirty-two grinned at me. "Well, into the wild blue yonder . . ." he whispered.

Summer raised an eyebrow. "He's real cute!"

I shrugged. "Not bad."

When our turn came, Summer and I rose side by side. She seemed to skim, to whirl, to swoop. A sea gull flying. I was sailing along beside her when suddenly my pilot light ignited and flared through my body, setting me free. I wasn't a bird. Not Cynthia Gregory, either. No, I was me. Lara Havas, a flame in the wind. Like Apa in Hungary years ago.

By the time we reached the opposite corner I was panting. I doubled over and gulped air. My ears blocked. I hung onto the barre to keep from falling. Summer collapsed beside me.

"I can't move," she moaned. "I'll die if we have to do it from the other side."

Fortunately, we didn't.

The way the pianist raced to the foyer, he seemed glad, too. But in the doorway he paused long enough to wink at me again.

"What? Another one?" Summer whispered. "Lord, that makes two. Shoot, girl, I've been wasting my time worrying about your heart being broken!"

"Well, it's not exactly mended yet," I said.

"That's it, ladies and gentlemen," Mr. Landon called. "We'll let you know in a few minutes." He joined the other judges at the table.

Waiting beside Summer, I used my towel to blot sweat off my neck and shoulders. When I saw Number Thirty-two heading my way, I turned toward the windows, unable right now to deal with him. Next thing I knew he was across the room talking to Number Nineteen and Meredith. Meredith! He seemed too nice a person to get mixed up with her!

I looked at the judges. What was taking them so long? Finally, Mr. Landon came toward us with a thin sheet of paper trembling in his hands.

"Will the following numbers please step to the center of the room?"

Among others, Summer's and Meredith's. Then mine! Summer's eyes grew shiny and uncertain. Meredith frowned. "We simply can't all be losers, can we?" she asked.

For a minute we stood there, tears running down our faces. Even Meredith's.

Mr. Landon said, "Get up here. Everybody whose number I called!"

Summer and I crept forward, followed by Meredith and a dozen or so other students, including Number Thirty-two.

"To you others," Mr. Landon said, "to those whose numbers weren't called, we want to thank you for coming. Not receiving a scholarship doesn't mean you aren't talented. It only means your type of dancer doesn't meet the needs —"

But I didn't hear the rest because happiness and excitement exploded inside me. Summer was hugging me and squealing in my ear. "We made it! We made it! The great team of Lara Havas and Summer Jones! Put her there, pardner!" We slapped palms.

Meredith ran up, laughing. "Well, I made it, too, you turkeys."

"We'll even press the flesh with you, creepy Meredith, won't we, Lara?" Summer said.

There was no way I could get out of it, but Summer did, because just then Jason pranced into the room. She dived into his arms and was lifted high in the air. Seeing them together brought back my ache for Peter.

Summer must have heard me sigh. "Are you okay, Lara?" she asked.

I nodded and was about to head for the

dressing room when Mrs. Martin strode smiling into the studio. I saw her stop abruptly and eye Summer and Jason. I expected fireworks, but she only shrugged.

"I give up," she said. "I guess you will have to learn the hard way, sweetheart." Then she laughed. "Just try not to do nothing I wouldn't, hear?"

I started. In all the years I had known Mrs. Martin I had never heard her use anything but perfect English.

Summer stared, then, giggling, she hugged Mrs. Martin. "Don't worry, Stephanie. Really. Jason and I plan to cool it."

"Hey, Lara. Hey, Lara," somebody was calling. I spun around and saw Number Thirty-two waving. Meredith must actually have told him my name. She and Number Nineteen waved, too.

"We're going out to celebrate," Number Thirty-two said. "Paint the Big Apple red! Want to come?"

"Sure, Lara, come on," Meredith said.

I shook my head. "Thanks a lot, all of you, but I'm sort of tired."

After they left, I walked to the windows and was staring out at the raw day when arms went around me from behind. Peter used to hug me like that. My heart jolted. But it was Stephanie Martin. She pulled me against her. Tears started down my cheeks.

"Take it easy," she said, patting my back. "I know how you feel. I've been there."

"Blackbird?" I asked.

She nodded. "That wasn't his name, though. It was the name of a song he wrote and I used to sing." Then, in a low haunting voice that sent shivers through me, she started crooning. *"Blackbird, Blackbird, singin' in some far tree! Ain'tcha never gone come home to me?*

"But someone else came along," she said, "and will for you, too, Lara. Someone older and more reliable and maybe less confused. So hang in there."

"I am."

"Good girl. I wanted to take all three of you out to tea, but Meredith and Summer made other plans. Especially Summer. Well, at least Jason is a dancer. Now get dressed and we'll go to the Russian Tea Room to celebrate the wonderful scholarship you won."

"I really got one, didn't I?" I said, smiling and wiping my eyes with a Kleenex she handed me.

"You did indeed, sweetheart."

I took a deep, shuddery breath and, looking out the window, saw that the rain had stopped. Through the grimy glass, sunlight came streaming. I had won a time to dance.

About the Author

Karen Strickler Dean has studied dance with Bronislava and Irina Nijinska at the San Francisco Ballet School, and has been a balletomane for 40 years. Other books by Karen Dean include *Maggie Adams, Dancer; Mariana,* and *Between Dances, Maggie Adams Eighteenth Summer.* Ms. Dean lives with her husband in Palo Alto, California.